MW01047245

Too Rich To Love

(A romantic comedy novel)

Pamela Osborne

PAVERS
Publishing

Too Rich To Love™
Published by Pavers Publishing, LLC
28211 Southfield Rd., #760152
Lathrup Village, MI 48076
www.PaversHomes.com.

ISBN 978-1-9389890-1-8
ISBN 978-1-9389890-2-5 (electronic)

Copyright © 2013 by Pamela Osborne

All rights reserved. No part of this book may be reproduced or transmitted in any form or by any means, electronic or mechanical, including photocopying and recording, or by any information storage and retrieval system, without permission in writing from the publisher, except in the case of brief quotations embodied in critical articles and reviews.

This is a work of fiction, characters, places, and incidents either are the product of the author's imagination or are used fictitiously. Any resemblance to actual events, locales, organizations, or persons, living or dead, is entirely coincidental and beyond the intent of either the author or the publisher. Pavers Publishing, LLC, takes no responsibility for the companies advertising in this book or on its websites, blogs, or any other means of communication, electronic or otherwise.

Pavers Publishing, LLC, Too Rich To Love, and Pavers Homes, are trademarks of Pamela Osborne.

Scripture quotations are taken from The Holy Bible, King James Version.

This book was revised and renamed from, "Bread and Butter," as published by Pavers Publishing in 2003.

Scripture quotations are taken from The Holy Bible, King James Version

Book cover and page design by Shannon Crowley,
Treasure Image & Publishing – TreasureImagePublishing.com

Editorial development by Minister Mary D. Edwards,
Leaves of Gold Consulting, LLC – LeavesOfGoldConsulting.com

Published in the United States of America by Pavers Publishing, LLC.
Printed in the United States of America

10 9 8 7 6 5 4 3 2 1

SPECIAL SALES
Most Pavers Publishing, LLC books are available at special quantity discounts when purchased in bulk by corporations, organizations, and special-interest groups. Custom imprinting or excerpting can also be done to fit special needs. For information please email info@pavershomes.com, or call (248) 809-5121. More Pavers Publishing, LLC books can be found at www.PaversHomes.com.

I dedicate this book to everyone who wants to laugh and love.

ACKNOWLEDGEMENTS

I'd like to acknowledge God for all His goodness toward me. I also want to thank my family and friends for their words of encouragement.

I'd also like to thank my special friend, Minister Mary Edwards, who helped edit this book and encouraged me in many ways. I also thank Rahijaa Freeman of Creative Buds Inc., for her creative, business and marketing acumen.

1

"Thanks for giving me a lift to the airport, boss. It saves me a lot of money. I'd spend a fortune if I had to park my car or take a taxi," Stewart Counts graciously acknowledged to his boss, Solomon Wise, nicknamed "Monzie." It was a warm and sunny Sunday, mid-afternoon in July as Monzie drove down I-94 from Detroit to the Detroit Metropolitan Wayne County Airport.

He was wearing an old thin-lapel, polyester, dark brown blazer over a white, heavy, long-sleeve t-shirt and light brown trousers that was short enough to see his thick white socks over his black vinyl shoes. The suit looked almost as old as he.

"My pleasure to be your chauffeur," Monzie obliged.

"Besides, this is the only way I can be sure you'll take a well needed vacation. You need to treat yourself after closing that $500 million real estate deal. Your lawyer skills saved us when the buyer threatened to pull out on the day of the closing." Monzie was fifty-seven. He was the owner and president of Detroit Prime Properties, Inc., the largest commercial real estate firm in Michigan.

Stewart took a deep breath, and then let it out of his five feet-eleven lean sun-deprived physique. "I was happy to handle the closing. Besides, there was no way I was going to let all that money walk out the door."

"Stewart, you were worth every penny of that $25

million dollar commission."

"Thanks Monzie. I'm going to make good use of it all, no thanks to the newspapers that put my name in the news as the one who closed the deal. I've gotten all kinds of calls and e-mails from strangers begging me for money, not to mention their wedding proposals! Relatives I never knew I had are asking me to invest in their hair-brained schemes. Let me tell you something, Monzie. I've got big plans for this money and they don't include anybody getting any of it."

"Money isn't everything. Sometimes man needs a little companionship. Besides, I doubt if a handsome 24-year-old and successful commercial real estate attorney like you will not be attractive to some women."

"That's their problem."

"Suit yourself. Here we are. My wife, kids and I are going to Europe for a week for some site-seeing. They tell me that Paris is lovely in July. We should be back by Friday. Do you think you'll need a lift when you return from Savannah, Georgia?"

"Yes. That would be nice. I couldn't think of anyone else to take Bread and I to the airport. On second thought, maybe I should cancel the whole thing. I don't take vacations."

"Bread does. You wouldn't want to disappoint him, would you?" Monzie looked at Bread, Stewart's chocolate brown Labrador retriever, as he kept unloading the luggage at the airport's departure section.

"You're right. This is about spending some quality time with my best friend. See you in a week. Thanks for the free ride."

"You're welcome. Bread, keep an eye out for my partner here." Monzie smiled and patted Bread on the head. Bread waved his tail.

Elsewhere, in a downtown Detroit high-rise luxury apartment, Deborah Dents asked herself, "Where are those tickets? I thought I placed them over here somewhere."

Her apartment intercom buzzer sounded.

A voice announced, "Ms. Dents, there's a gentleman here to see you. His name is Will. Shall I send him up?"

"Yes. Thank you, Mr. Gaiter. Send him up please," Debbie said to the doorman.

Will, Debbie's older brother, knocked on her door. She hurriedly let him in.

"How are you doing, Sis? Get a move on. You never know if we'll run into construction or delays on the freeway."

"I'm doing great, Will. I'll be much better when I find my plane ticket to Savannah. Please load the car while I continue to look. Can you also carry Butter out to the car for me?"

"Okay. I'll be happy to. Come on, Butter. I know you'll be a good cat on this trip," he assured the frisky cat as they walked down the hallway to the elevator.

"Great. Here are my tickets in my tote bag, right where I left them."

The phone rang just before she left the apartment.

"Hello?"

"Hello. I love you darling. I love you so much, Debbie. I'm really sorry about our last date. I realized that I tried to go too far with you last year. I'll never hit you again. Please, please, take me back," her ex-boyfriend, George, pleaded and sobbed as she listened.

"No, George! I told you that I don't want to see or hear from you again. It's over, and I do mean over. One more call from you and I'll call the police." Then she hung up the phone without giving him an opportunity to say another word.

By this time, Will returned on the up elevator to see what was taking her so long. He saw Debbie down the hallway about to lock the door to her apartment. "Come on, let's go, Debbie. The plane leaves for Savannah at 3:30 p.m., and I'm sure Butter will be very disappointed if she doesn't start her vacation at the Pets-by-the-Sea Hotel today." He held the elevator door for her until the buzzer went off. He apologized to the stranger on the elevator.

"Excuse me, sir, I didn't mean to hold the elevator door that long. I'll get off."

Butter hissed at the stranger.

The stranger stared at Will intensely as Will disembarked.

"Let's go. Let's go," Will coaxed Debbie in a friendly voice.

"I'm ready for this trip. The sooner I get out of town, the better," a flustered Debbie said as they rushed to the car.

Will drove Debbie and Butter down I-94 from Detroit to the Airport.

"Sis, I want you to enjoy this trip. I know how hard you've worked for a solid year on that mansion's interior design project. So relax, have some fun."

"I wish somebody from my family was coming with me."

Debbie caught a glimpse of Butter as she spoke. "No

offense, Butter. I'll have fun with you."

Butter looked up at Debbie.

"Maybe you'll meet someone there to share some of your time." Will suggested.

"I don't date any more. I have done enough of that now that I am twenty-four and a very successful interior designer. I don't need a man to take care of me. In fact, the last thing I want is a man." Debbie fidgeted, brushing her sleeves with her hands.

"You mean like George?" Will asked.

"Yes. That was George who just called me. Can you imagine that?"

"Debbie, is he bothering you again?"

"Not really. I hadn't heard from that man in a year. I definitely made it clear that if I hear from him again, I'll call the police."

"Let me know if he tries to talk to you again. You know your big brother will take care of him real good."

"Thanks, but no thanks. He's not worth going to jail over. Besides, I've taken a few karate lessons since then. I guarantee you that I can handle any situation involving 'fresh' men very well."

"Like when you went on a date last month with what's his- name, Ralph?"

Laughing very hard, relaxing her tense muscles, she responded, "You mean errrRalph?" Debbie tried to imitate a growling sound the way Ralph liked to introduce himself.

Will laughed.

"Didn't he want to make music with you all night long? Then you told him you liked 'Chopsticks' and gave him a karate chop?" They both chuckled.

"I'm not taking any chances with these guys. If a man looks at me the wrong way, he's in for a rude awakening."

"Sis, not all men are dogs. Some are gentle and kind like your brother."

"I know. But until I figure out the gentle from the rough, I'm going to continue working on getting my black belt."

"Finally, we're here. Here comes the sky captain for Butter and you."

"Thanks so much for taking us to the airport, Will. Love ya. I'll call you when I get to the hotel."

"That's what big brothers are for, my dear. Love you too, Debbie. See you in a week."

2

Debbie took a big sigh. At last it was a relief to board the plane from Detroit, Michigan to Savannah, Georgia and relax. All day she had been in a rush-rush mode. Pushing her hair back from her face, she saw her seat, "Excuse me, sir," she politely stated and motioned for the guy to let her in.

"Of course." Stewart promptly let her through to the window seat.

She almost touched him as she quickly moved to sit down.

He glanced at her soft tresses that hung loosely around her pretty oval face. She could hear him take in a deep breath of her perfume. A smile crept across his face. Slightly bending over, she positioned her large tote bag under the seat in front of her, after taking a book out of it to read.

She quickly took a side-glance at his left hand ring finger. He wasn't wearing a wedding ring. She glanced at him. He glanced at her. They glanced away.

Stewart began reading a magazine, and then glanced at Debbie's legs. She was wearing a long sleeve, ankle length, cream colored, cotton dress. She was pretty much covered from head to toe. Going through the motions of flipping the magazine's pages, his eyes moved downward to her feet and the pumps she was wearing that matched her dress.

Looking out of the side of her eye again, while

turning the pages of her book about home designs, she observed that he was wearing some old khaki brown pants and black shoes.

The flight attendant checked the seatbelts of the passengers as she moved down the aisle. "That's right sir. Buckle up like that," the attendant said to Stewart.

The flight attendant walked down the aisle with the beverage cart. As she approached Stewart and Debbie she asked, "Would you like a beverage?"

"How much does it cost?" Stewart inquired.

"No charge, sir. Would you like one?"

In a very kind tone he asked, "Do you have ginger ale?"

"Yes, we do."

"I'll have that. Thanks," he stated with a big smile.

"And you, ma'am? What would you like?"

"A bottle of non-flavored water is fine," she replied.

"Right here."

"Thank you," she said to the attendant.

"How about a turkey sandwich?" the flight attendant asked Stewart.

"How much does it cost?" he asked.

"No charge, sir," replied the attendant.

"And you, ma'am? Would you like a sandwich?"

"I'll have a cheese sandwich, please. May I have a blanket also?"

"Sure thing. I'll get one for you in a jiffy."

3

The plane landed in Savannah. As the cargo door opened, the cargo crew unloaded the pet cages and luggage.

Stewart reached the luggage and pets-pick-up area.

"Hi Bread. That was a great flight, wasn't it?" He grabbed his luggage and Bread in the cage then proceeded directly outside to catch a shuttle to the hotel.

"Hi, are you Stewart Counts? This must be Bread, from the description you gave us. I'm the shuttle driver, Timothy. I'll take you and your pet to the Pets-by-the-Sea Hotel. Our shuttle is right here, all set to go."

"Thank you. We're ready. Do you work for the hotel?" Stewart asked.

"Just for the summer, before I start college this fall."

Shortly thereafter, Timothy sees Debbie.

"Ms. Dent?" Timothy asked.

"Yes I am," Debbie replied.

"Is this little Butter?"

"She sure is."

"Right this way to the shuttle."

Debbie and Butter boarded the shuttle to the hotel.

Soon they were all at the hotel. Timothy unloaded the luggage at the hotel's entrance.

"Thanks," Stewart said, without giving Timothy a tip.

"What a beautiful entrance, Bread. Look, they even have a gray statue of a Labrador Retriever holding a flower basket with fresh cut flowers."

"Welcome to Pets-by-the-Sea Hotel. Your name please?"

Martha, the front desk clerk, greeted him. She was a full-figured woman and was wearing a starchy buttoned-to-the-neck white blouse, under a straight line, no-nonsense black business suit.

She wore a short Afro, which framed her square-shaped honey-tone face.

"Hello. It's Stewart Counts and my dog's name is Bread."

"Is that spelled 'b-r-e-a-d' as in 'bread and butter'?"

"Yes. That's how it's spelled."

"I see your reservation right here. We have you in the best room for dogs in the hotel. If you'll sign right here, Mr. Counts, someone will take you to your room."

"Thank you."

"The dining room is closed for the night. However, we have 24-hour, free room service," she explained. Bread looked up at her from his cage, as she leaned over and smiled at him.

Martha continued, "There's one very important rule here. When you're in the lobby with your pet, it must always be on a leash. There are no exceptions to this rule because it's for the safety of the pet and others."

"Yes. I'll see to that," Stewart responded. As he walked through the lobby, he was engrossed with the décor. Paintings and photos of pets lined the walls. There were photographs of some famous individuals, along with their pets, hanging on the walls. Then he commented absently to Bread, "This picture is my favorite of Jesus holding a little lamb. The subtitle says: 'It is not the will of your Father, which is in heaven, that one of these little ones should perish. Matthew 18:14.' Here's another peaceful scene of Jesus with animals. 'The wolf shall also dwell with the lamb, and the leopard shall lie down with the kid; and the calf and the young lion and the fatling together; and a little child shall lead them. Isaiah 11:6-7.'"

Stewart observed the custom-designed carpeting. It was picturesque with a variety of birds, fish and other animal motifs interspersed. Elegant ribbons and gold medallions were geometrically placed in a checkered pattern. Many pets in wheeled cages or leashes were coming and going with their owners through the lobby on their way to their rooms. Murals framed the archway of the two halls, which led to corridors where the guest rooms were located.

"Do you have a lot of religious retreats here?" he asked Martha.

"No, we don't. The owner, David Shepherd, is an ordained minister who strongly feels that biblical history and art go hand in hand."

On one side of the lobby was the archway to the Cat Wing.

The mural contained a variety of feline species strategically placed around the archway. On the opposite side of the lobby was the Dog Wing with a large mural of many breeds of dogs also placed on the archway. Facing the front desk was the corridor that led to restaurants, a pet salon, a pet gift shop, and pet exercise rooms.

Other amenities were a vet station, a pet sitter room, and a small chapel where owners could pray with their pets. This extra-large center archway was framed with all kinds of pets that people have been known to own such as gerbils, hamsters, rabbits, birds, fish, turtles and pigs. They were arranged like a chorus, in tiers of smiling animals, to welcome all visitors.

As they approached the Dog Wing, Stewart pointed to a mural on the wall of a chocolate Labrador Retriever that resembled Bread. The room numbers on each door was attached to what looked like a dog's bowl.

4

Stewart and Bread were settling down in their room.

"This hotel room is like dog heaven. Look Bread, they've prepared a plate of dog food and a bowl of water for you and there's a guest basket of snacks, fruit, and an assortment of beverages for me."

Bread went straight to the food and started to eat.

The room was decorated in cool colors. The soothing, pale blue and green walls looked like a watermark. A variety of breeds of dogs were designed in the curtains, bedspread, and upholstery fabric.

"I like the décor too. What about you, Bread?"

Bread showed his approval by sniffing the room over after eating.

The décor was elegant, from top to bottom. The shower curtains had dog patterns with a seashore background. The toilet seat cover was patterned with pictures of dogs. The little bathroom cups were stenciled in varied dog toy designs, like toy bones and biscuits. The clock on the wall was shaped like a dog with the tail wagging as the clock's motions reflected the seconds. At six p.m., the clock barked time like a puppy.

"Do you think the decorator liked dogs?" Stewart teased Bread.

After eating some dog food, Bread ran over to the patio door. Stewart could see the large enclosed high fenced patio where Bread could relieve himself. He let

19

him out and a few yards away, someone snapped a picture of the patio. Bread looked at the person and the person looked at Bread before moving on without saying a word. Bread took a moment to eliminate.

Within minutes, a groundskeeper came by and used a long handled scooper to remove the waste, then quietly moved on to the next patio yard.

Outside on the patio, Stewart noticed that his room overlooked the waterfront. "Whoa. Look at this view."

Then he settled in for a few refreshments as he unpacked his luggage.

While relaxing in the dog-shaped easy chair that had a slightly elevated lounging dog bed by it, Stewart looked around the room. He picked up the remote control and flipped on the TV. The TV was programmed to the Pets-N-Things station that was available to watch 24-hours a day. This particular program was about antique pet-shaped ceramics. He flipped to the internal hotel channel showing activities planned for the week.

"Let's see, what's for tomorrow? The travel package included activities. Might as well get our money's worth." He scrolled down to Monday's agenda. "There's a boat tour off the coast of Georgia. That looks like fun. I'll call right now to reserve us a spot."

He reached for the poodle-shaped phone, located in the built-in armrest of his easy chair. "Hello, this is Stewart Counts. I'd like to make reservations for Bread and I to go on the boat ride tomorrow. Thanks. Good-bye."

He pushed a button that electronically caused his easy chair's backrest to lean back as it lifted the leg rest up. As his eyes turned to the shell-white ceiling he noticed faint watermarks like off-white figures of angels with wings. "This is really living," he said with a relaxing sigh. "What more could I ask for?"

Bread was fast asleep now.

"That sleep looks good to me, Bread. I think I'd better turn in early so that we won't miss that free room service before the boat ride."

5

Debbie was next to being waited on at the Hotel registration desk.

"Welcome to the Pets-By-The-Sea Hotel. I hope your stay will be enjoyable," greeted Martha from the front desk.

"Thank you, I hope so too," Debbie replied.

She turned around as her eyes quickly glanced at the interior design of the lobby. She shook her head and muttered, "This is going to be different."

"Let's see our room, Butter." She pulled out her camera midway through the large lobby. "The designers back home will never believe this," Debbie said as she shuttered away taking pictures of the unusual murals. While walking through the lobby to her room she asked Timothy, "Who is the hotel's interior designer?"

"You like it? We're quite proud of it. I believe the theme of the animals and stuff is from our hotel owner, Mr. Shepherd, who thought of it. We didn't use a professional designer."

"Figures...uh, I mean, that's very original," Debbie said catching her words.

"Thanks. I'll tell him you like it. Some people make jokes about it. However, most of our visitors just get used to it after a few days," Timothy chirped.

"That's nice."

Just as they were halfway across the lobby, there was a loud rushing sound. The other pets were hovering close to their owners.

"Yip!" one woman shouted. "What's that?" another woman shouted, while climbing on a table nearby.

"Get it! Do something!" a man shouted.

In a split second Martha rushed from around the front desk to chase a small creature dashing along the floor near the sides of the wall. In another split second, she overtook it as it tried to figure out which way to turn, with its tail down along the side of its body, against the wall. It let out a desperate squeak and squeal. "Plop! Slam! Stomp," Martha went with her shoe, still on her foot, on the little critter.

"Everything is fine. It's all taken care of," Martha assured all of the guests, who were frozen in fear.

Debbie looked from a distance and saw a lifeless field mouse lying on the floor.

"How do you know that this wasn't someone's pet?" Debbie asked while still in shock.

"It wasn't on a leash," the matter-of-fact Martha answered, as she returned to the front desk like nothing happened.

"Timothy," Martha called.

"Yes, Ms. Martha."

"When you return from taking Ms. Dents to her room, dispose of it."

"Yes, ma'am," Timothy humbly replied. As Debbie and Timothy entered the corridor where Debbie was staying, out of sight of Martha, Timothy explained, "Ms. Martha is very strict about those things. Her motto is, 'No Pay, No Play.'"

Sensing Debbie's uneasiness, he added, "but she's really a nice person once you get to know her."

She kept walking but held Butter tighter.

Back in the lobby, someone took a picture of the now expired field mouse.

"Here's your room," Timothy said, opening the door to Debbie's room. "Butter should perk up when she gets a look at her room. Enjoy your stay."

"Thank you. I think everything will be all right. I hope. Here's your tip."

The time on the clock turned to 8 p.m. and the kitten shaped wall clock let out a pleasant sounding kitten meow.

Debbie carried Butter in her arms as she walked around the room to look around. The décor was cats and kittens. Cat patterns were on the bedspread, curtains, draperies and towels, everywhere.

Butter squirmed until Debbie put her down. Butter proceeded directly to the food and dug in.

Debbie laughed.

Opening the patio drapes, she could see the enclosed high fenced-in yard. They had lounge chairs, upholstered in a cat pattern. When she turned back to the interior room, she glanced over to the table that had a gift basket on it. She opened it and looked inside to find some very nice snacks. She took pictures of the room to show to her designer friends and family back home. After freshening up in the bathroom she called back home to her brother, Will.

"Hi, Will. I've arrived at the hotel and want to give you my number."

"How was the trip, Sis?"

"Fine. The room appears to be very nice, although I might have toned down some of the cat-themed things."

Will laughed. "Remember you're there to relax and enjoy yourself. No interior design work."

"Yes, big brother. See you in a week."

"Have some fun. Pick up a guy or two, not literally of course," Will inferred, jokingly.

"With all these animals around here, not a chance," Debbie laughed.

"Good-bye," Will laughed back.

"Love ya."

"Me too."

Debbie started to eat some snacks from the fruit and snack basket. Glancing for something to read, she found a magazine and settled in. There were cat litter pans outside and inside. Debbie had a full view of the patio from her chair, so she let Butter out.

After a few minutes, Debbie waved to Butter, "Come on back into the room Butter. It's getting dark out there." Butter scampered back into the room. Debbie drew the draperies and turned on the TV.

"Look Butter. There's a channel about pets and animals. How interesting. What other channels do they have? This is the hotel information channel. Let's see what's scheduled for Monday? There's a boat ride for guests and pets. Won't that be fun?"

"I know you don't like water, but you won't get a drop on you. We'll be on this nice large boat. It's so hot down here that the cool breeze from the ocean should be very energizing.

Besides, I'll always be with you." Debbie stroked

Butter's fur.

"I'll check the front desk to see if they have any room left."

"Hello. Are many people going on the boat ride tomorrow?"

"We're almost full. Would you like to reserve two seats?

It's part of the package," Martha offered.

"Yes. It sounds like fun. Thank you."

"You're welcome."

While Butter was preoccupied with the toy, Debbie got ready for bed. Just before she turned out the light she reached for the Bible in the nightstand beside her. She allowed the pages to fall open as she looked inside and read Matthew 6:34: *"Take therefore no thought for the morrow; for the morrow shall take thought for the things of itself. Sufficient unto the day is the evil thereof."*

6

Back in Detroit, Gloria Harps asked her friend, Sharon Love, "Do you think this gold iridescent lipstick is sexy enough? Never mind. You can drop me off at that flight departure door."

"Are you sure about this? Need I remind you that you're Stewart's secretary, and you could lose your job over this adventure?" Sharon Love was Gloria's best friend and the travel agent that arranged the trips for Gloria and Stewart.

"He's worth the risk. Besides, I can spend my $10,000 bonus check from the real estate deal anyway I please."

"Here's your ticket, itinerary, and confirmation numbers for Savannah."

"Thanks for the lift, Sharon."

"Here's your luggage, Gloria. Are you really sure about this? Stewart will be shocked to see his secretary at the same hotel," she asked again.

"It's the only way I can spend some time with him away from work. He's a workaholic. He seldom notices me or any woman."

"Okay. I just don't want you to get rejected like you have in the past."

"I've spent all weekend buying sexy clothes and make-up. I just didn't show enough stuff with the other men."

"Did they tell you that?" Sharon questioned.

"Not exactly. But all men want is what they see, and Stewart's going to see a lot of me in Savannah."

Gloria was Stewart's 28-years-old secretary. She had an ample bust line and curvy hips. Her highlighted brownish red, full-bodied curly hair had overtones of shimmering shades of gold. It hung several inches below her shoulders and was layered for fullness and body. Her big brown eyes shone with excitement from the golden glitter she wore on her eyelids and cheeks. Her four-inch dangling, beaded earrings in metallic gold sequins matched the several glittering gold bracelets and anklets. Coppery red lip pencil and gold gloss slathered her lips. Wearing a gold, sequined, low cut tank top, with matching gold chiffon mini-skirt, she looked like a model on a hip-hop magazine cover. Her hosiery even glistened with threads of gold. Her shoes were 4-inch high heel gold leather sandals with thin ankle straps that tied in a bow in the back. A little glitter donned her bare shoulders.

"Here's your boarding pass, Ms. Harps. You are in seat 44A and can board now." The ticket agent pointed to the boarding gate.

"Thanks."

Ralph Rolls, another Detroiter, stood at the same airport reservation counter and asked, "Got any seats on the plane going to Savannah, Georgia?"

"Do you have a reservation?" the agent routinely asked.

"If I had a reservation I wouldn't be asking if you have any seats, now would I?" Ralph retorted impatiently.

"Let me check the computer. It looks as if we may

have one seat left," the irritated agent replied.

"I'll take it."

"I need your picture ID, please."

"The name is errrRalph Rolls, as in 'I'd like to roll with you, babe.'"

The agent gave him a raised eyebrow and stern look. Ralph was 5'7' and 30. He sported a stylish multi-length short black haircut and a muscular rugged body.

"Any luggage?" she asked.

"I have a set of drums. I need to take them on the plane with me."

Looking over the counter at a full scale set of drums, the agent warned, "I'm sorry Mr. Rolls, your drums need packaging for travel. I can get our shipping and handling department to package them for you."

"What am I going to do without my drums?"

"How about staying home? Just joking. You can get them shipped on a later flight."

"I'm not taking a ship. I'm taking an airplane."

"Which is it, Mr. Rolls? Are you staying here with the drums or leaving without them? The plane is leaving in 15 minutes."

"If I had more time, I'd see the manager about this. Say, Ethan," motioning his younger brother and fellow band member to come closer to him. "Do me a favor, little brother.

Keep my drums at your place until I return. I'll see you when I get back from Savannah."

"Sure thing, Ralph, but I really don't think this is a good idea, following Debbie after what she did to you the last time."

"That was nothing. Look, man, I've got to follow my dreams and my heart," Ralph explained as he held his right hand over the left side of his chest.

"Is there any other luggage, sir?" the agent interrupted.

"No. Wait. Just my drumsticks, if you think they will fit under the seat," Ralph said sarcastically.

"You'll have to check them, sir," the agent glibly informed.

"Why?"

Without answering, the agent looked at her watch.

"Here they are."

"Have you been asked to bring those drumsticks by anyone, or have they ever been out of your view at anytime, sir?"

"No. Yes. Every time I look at your pretty face, you pretty thing you," Ralph grinned.

"Here is your baggage claim ticket and boarding pass, you will be in seat number 41C. Enjoy your flight," the agent continued, without acknowledging Ralph's last remark.

"Take care of my drums while I'm gone," Ralph said as he tossed the keys to his new SUV to his brother.

"Gee, thanks," Ethan said while catching the keys. "What about the band?" Ethan asked.

"I know you're a very responsible kid, so you can handle that too. I'll call you to pick me up when I get back."

With the ticket in one hand, Ralph took a minute to check out the clerk's nice legs as she turned around to place his drumsticks on the baggage conveyer belt. "Not bad. Say, pretty thing, want to join me? I'll take you on a flight you've never been on before." Ralph said, trying to flirt with the clerk.

"Next customer, please."

He hurried through the security check to board the plane. Walking down the narrow aisle, he noticed that his seat was next to an elderly man. Looking around to see if a better seat was available, he spotted one by a pretty young woman. He checked his ticket seat number again and pulled out his black ink pen, changed the 41C to a 44B. He then politely sat down by the young lady. Just as he was buckling his seatbelt, a young teenage boy assigned to 44B approached with his ticket in hand.

"Excuse me sir, I think you are in my seat. I'm assigned to seat 44B," the boy said holding up his boarding pass.

"That can't be. My ticket says 44B, see?" Ralph said flashing his ticket quickly.

"Let me see that again."

Just then the flight attendant announced, "Our flight will be departing on schedule in two minutes. Passengers, please take your seats." She looked straight at the teenage boy standing in the aisle.

The boy tried to wait to explain some more to Ralph.

"You heard the attendant. Look. Take that seat up there.

Now go go go, before she kicks you off the plane for disturbing me."

The young fellow quickly took seat 41C.

Settling down into his seat, Ralph returned his eyes to the lovely lady next to him. "Hi. I'm errrRalph, and your name is?"

Gloria took one look at Ralph and said, "Do I know you?"

"Yes. We met, you know, it's on the tip of my tongue."

"Let it stay there. I saw what you did when you changed your seat number. You've got a lot of nerve telling that young kid he had the wrong seat. We're grown adults. We're supposed to set an example for young people."

"Look lady, if you are so high and mighty, why are you dressed like a hooker?"

"What did you say?" Gloria fumed.

"Looker. I said you dress like a looker."

"Get lost," she said as she turned her back to Ralph, fluffed up her pillow and pretended to get some sleep.

With her back turned, along with the rest of her body he noticed her curvy hips.

"Got a sister?" he asked.

"If I did, you'd never know it," she mumbled with her back still turned.

"I just asked so that I'd have to turn her down if she came on to me like you," he chimed.

"If you say one more word to me, I'm going to tell the attendant what you did," she replied, letting him know that she meant business.

Deciding to drop the conversation, he mumbled, "It's going to be a long flight."

Neither she nor he uttered a word to each other for the duration of the flight. Gloria relaxed with her eyes still shut.

Ralph silently patted out new drumbeats with his

fingers on a pillow until he dozed off to sleep.

"We'll be landing on schedule in Savannah at 10 p.m. The temperature in Savannah is 85 degrees. We hope you enjoyed your flight with us," said the pilot over the speakers.

"Yeah, charming," Ralph snarled after waking up from a brief nap just in time to unbuckle his seat belt and deplane.

Likewise, Gloria eagerly gathered her purse and carry-on baggage. She headed to the baggage claim. Ralph quickly spotted his drumsticks on the baggage conveyer belt. Gloria grabbed her luggage, then proceeded to the bus shuttle loading area for the ride to the hotel. He hailed a cab.

"Where to, sir?" the cab driver asked.

"Someplace that has pets," Ralph directed.

"I beg your pardon, sir? Where do you want to go?" the driver asked again.

"You know. Don't you have a hotel for pets around here?" he inquired.

"You mean the Pets-by-the-Sea Hotel?"

"Yeah, yeah. That's the one. And don't take the long way. I know my way around here."

"Yes, sir," the cab driver answered, slightly shaking his head.

7

It wasn't long before Gloria arrived at the Pets-by-the-Sea Hotel on the hotel shuttle. It arrived at the hotel the same time that Ralph arrived in the cab.

"Hello. May I help you?" Martha asked.

"Yes. I want a room," Ralph replied.

When Gloria approached the front desk, she looked up and saw Ralph. Throwing her hair back, she piped in, "I have reservations."

"Are you together?" Martha asked.

"No way," she said.

"Your names?" Martha asked.

"Gloria Harps."

"Ralph Rolls."

Martha checked the reservations. "I only see a reservation for Gloria Harps. The pet listed is a cat named 'Jazzy.' Where is the cat?"

Bending over in her gold-toned mini-skirt and low-cut halter, front first, she began to look in her tote bag. Ralph was taking a good look at her cleavage. She reached into her tote bag and pulled out a large stuffed silver fur toy cat with a red bow and label that read, "Jazzy." She sat it on the counter and said, "That's Jazzy."

"I'm sorry. We don't check in stuffed pets."

"What difference does it make? It's not like they're paying the bill," she pleaded.

"It's our hotel policy. While you are figuring that out, let me look up this gentleman's name." She looked for the name on the computer for several minutes, but didn't see it.

Ralph was standing there, still looking over Gloria. She looked away, then at her watch.

Martha continued checking the card index as well as the daily computer printout. "I don't see your name, sir. Did you get a confirmation number?"

"What for? I didn't make a reservation. I want a room."

Martha began to tighten her lips.

"I see. There's one room left. By the way, what pet would you be bringing?" Martha looked around Ralph for a pet.

He spotted a fly on the counter nearby, grabbed a newspaper that was sitting on the counter and in a split second, swatted the fly with the paper.

"There's my pet," Ralph said with a grin, pointing at the squashed fly still on the paper.

"We only accept live pets. Besides, that's a pest and they aren't allowed," Martha sternly stated. She looked straight at Ralph as she grabbed the paper and tossed it in the trash basket.

"I don't have a pet, ma'am. However, I can pay you a little extra, if you let me slide."

"Sir, that won't be necessary. You must either have a domesticated or common household pet."

Gloria surmised, "There is no way I'm going home

before I accomplish my mission. Is there a pet store nearby? All I need is a pet and I'll get my room?"

"That is correct. No pet stores are open after 10 p.m. on a Sunday night. The only thing open is U-Save on the outskirts of the city."

"Call us a cab. We're going shopping," Ralph replied in a bossy manner.

"We? I'm not going anywhere with you," Gloria protested.

"We'll both be out on the streets without a pet," Ralph reasoned.

"Madam, why are you standing there? Call a cab... please," Ralph spoke to Martha.

Martha proceeded to call a cab.

"I'll split the tab," nonchalantly he stated to Gloria.

"What? I'm not getting in a cab with you."

Within minutes a cab arrived.

"Here's our cab," Ralph said, motioning Gloria to join him.

"You don't get it. This cab is for me," Gloria complained.

"Look sweetheart, there's one cab. I asked for it, not you. Now you can stand here on the curb or join me," Ralph said, giving her an ultimatum.

"Okay. U-Save, please," she said to the cab driver as she motioned for Ralph to sit in the back seat.

"Sure thing," the cab driver replied.

One hour later they returned to the hotel.

"Here are my pets. I have two goldfish because I wanted them to have company." Gloria placed them, still in the plastic bag, on the counter as proof.

"Very well. What are their names?" Martha inquired.

"Goldie."

"And the other one?" Martha asked.

"Since they'll always be together, I gave them the same name, Goldie."

"Okay, Ms. Harps. Here are your keys. Since you registered for a cat, the only room we have for you is in a cat room."

"But I wanted to be near the dogs," she disappointedly groaned.

"You're standing by one, aarrf, aarrf," Ralph yipped while making a sweet puppy face.

Gloria shook her head in disgust and looked around impatiently for the bellhop.

Just then Timothy came and took Gloria's luggage. Carrying her goldfish, she followed him to her room.

"Here's your room, ma'am." Timothy opened the door to her room and placed the luggage on the rack. "I believe there is a guest here by the name of Stewart Counts. Can you slip this under his door tonight?"

"Certainly. Have a good evening," Timothy obliged.

"Thanks. Please don't tell him where it came from. It's a surprise. Here's your tip." She closed the door behind him and got ready for bed.

Ralph was still standing at the front desk trying to get a room. "Here you go. I have a parakeet. I'll take that room now, toots."

"The name is Martha. That will be $10,000 for the week, please."

"For what? I'm not buying the place. I'm renting a room," Ralph objected.

"That's for the all-inclusive package. We will reimburse your flight expenses. That also includes all the activities and food."

"I didn't come here to participate in hotel activities or eat food and I've already paid for my plane ticket," Ralph protested.

"Then why did you come?"

"To see your smiling face."

Martha stood in silence.

"What other kinds of packages do you have?"

"That's it. Everything else is ala carte for walk-ins, which could run you up to $20,000, depending on what you eat and do. Which do you want?"

Ralph looked in his wallet and saw only a few hundred dollars. "I was in a rush and left my money at home. Do you take Visa, Master Charge, American Express and Diners Club?"

Ralph laid all four cards on the counter.

Martha gathered them up and proceeded to add the hotel bill to each one up to their limit, until it totaled $10,000.

"What's your pet's name?" she asked.

"Which one? Oh, you mean my pet here. He's been talking ever since I got him. How about 'Talker?'"

"Here you are, sir. Just sign each one of these credit charges. No loose birds allowed. Talker must be in a cage when in the lobby at all times," Martha warned.

"I know one bird in this lobby that I'd like to put in a cage and throw away the key," he said sarcastically, looking straight at Martha.

She stared back at him and without a blink of her eyes sternly said, "Why would you lock yourself in a cage?"

He shook his head but kept silent.

She motioned with her hands for Timothy to come and escort Ralph to his room.

Timothy took Ralph and his parakeet to his room. "Do you have any luggage, sir?"

"Just my drumsticks and some clothes I grabbed from USave. You can carry everything but my drumsticks."

"Yes sir. What a pretty green and yellow bird."

"Yeah. Fine. Now go. I've got things to do." Ralph shushed Timothy out of the room after giving him a tip. He threw his drumsticks on the bed and then headed outdoors. He strolled around the hotel grounds.

Butter heard a noise. She jumped from her cat bed to look out the patio door.

"Meow, meow, meow." Butter raised her back until the hairs stood up as she hissed at the sight of Ralph. "Meow, meow, meow."

Ralph ran off before Debbie went to the patio.

"Butter, what is it?" Debbie said, rubbing her eyes as she looked out of her patio door.

"I don't see anything. What's wrong, Butter? A little critter scared you?"

Butter hissed.

"Come away from the patio door, Butter. Lie down and get some rest. We've got a big day tomorrow." Debbie comforted Butter by patting her on the head to calm her down.

8

"Hello. This is your wake up call, Mr. Counts. It's 7:00 a.m. We hope you and Bread had a restful night."

"Yes, we did, thank you. Thanks for the call."

"Have a great Monday!"

Stewart started his daily routines by reading the Bible. "Look at this, Bread." Stewart read First Thessalonians 5:6: *"Let us not sleep, as do others; but let us watch and be sober."*

"It says be alert."

Bread nodded in agreement.

"Okay, Bread. We've got to get moving. The boat leaves at nine." Stewart got up to let Bread out on the patio. The hotel had placed fresh food and water for him just outside the patio door. Bread ran straight to it and started eating. Stewart turned around to head for the bathroom. Suddenly, he saw an envelope on the floor by the hallway door. The smell of strong perfume hit him as he bent down to pick it up. "Mmm, nice. Who left this?" He read, *"'I've been waiting so long for this moment. Your Secret Admirer.'* Look at this, Bread. I wonder who sent it? Whoever she is smells nice," as he raised the envelope one more time to his nose. "What do you think, Bread?" He let Bread get a whiff of the envelope.

"I don't know anyone in Savannah that could have possibly done it. I sure hope it wasn't a gold digger," Stewart conjectured. "Enough of this. It's time to get going." Stewart laid out his very casual no-name and very outdated pants and t-shirt from the Second-Hand Store.

Gloria called Stewart on the telephone.

"Hello? Hello? Hello?" Stewart listened for a voice. "They hung up. Didn't say a word. Must have been a wrong number," Stewart surmised.

"Good. I know he made it to the hotel," Gloria said to herself from her hotel room after hanging up the telephone. She then rolled over and went back to sleep.

Debbie's room phone rang. Very sleepy, she rolled over, reached for the phone and was barely able to say, "Hello."

"Good morning, Ms. Dents, this is your wake up call. It's 8 a.m. We hope you and your pet had a restful night."

"Yes. Thanks." Debbie hung up the phone.

"Butter, we've got to get dressed and out of here by nine," she said as she rushed to the bathroom. In a few minutes, she was out of the bathroom and dressed in couture khaki designer jeans and a crisp white cotton shirt. She put on classic white sandals with a matching purse, and a large single pearl on a thin 14-karat gold strand necklace with a matching pearl earring set. "Come on. Let's go. We don't want to miss that boat," she said grabbing Butter with one arm and opening the room door to the corridor with the other.

"Welcome aboard," Mrs. Abigail Shepherd greeted Stewart, who was one of the first arrivals for the boat tour. She was a pretty and petite woman, whose face seemed to glow with enthusiasm, as it was encircled by her honey-brown hair in a short pixie haircut, fluffed up loosely. She was also the wife of Mr. David Shepherd, the owner/manager of the hotel. They were both in their mid-fifties. Their one son was 17-year-old Timothy, the bellhop/shuttle driver. Abby was in charge of planning all the hotel activities, programs and events. "Your names, please?" Abby asked Stewart.

"I made reservations by phone last night for Bread and myself, Stewart," he explained.

"Let me check the list. Yes. You are on the first level, stall 13 over there," Abby pointed.

"I'm Abby, the activities director. If you have any concerns regarding the programs and events, just let me know."

An announcement came over the loudspeaker for everyone on the boat to hear. "Good Morning. This is Captain Andrew. Welcome to the Fellowship, the only cruise boat of its kind, designed with pets and people in mind. The Fellowship is a special double-deck cruise boat, built especially for the safety of you and your dear pets. The upper deck is custom made for cats and other small creatures. The lower deck is designed for dogs, donkeys, pigs and other larger pets. The rails are spaced, so that pets of every size can get a good view of the ocean and beach. The fenced-in mesh panels prevent pets from slipping in between the railings."

"We are very proud of our safety record on the boat, having never lost a pet at sea, nor humans for that matter. The nonskid rubberized decks give our passengers sure footing to avoid sliding, slipping and falling. There are attached stall-gates that swing out and partitions to help separate the pets. Each stall has a hooking lock so that the pet can be attached by his leash or cage. We only ask that you observe two of our most important rules, which are, 1. All pets with leashes must be connected to the stall's hook at all times during the cruise and 2. No one, including pets, is allowed to lean over the railings. We truly hope that you will enjoy your tour on the Fellowship."

"Excuse, me," Debbie said, who was almost out of breath from running to the boat with Butter in hand. "Where do we sit?"

"You just made it. Another minute and you would have missed the boat. Your names please?" Abby inquired.

"I'm Debbie and this is Butter."

"Yes. I see your names. Go straight up there to the upper level. Stall number 23."

Just then the boat blew a loud horn as it signaled its departure.

"Let's hurry, Butter, we don't want to miss the view."

Debbie rushed up the stairs before Abby could explain the safety rules.

The boat was pulling away from the shore now. Debbie and Butter reached their stall. Debbie settled into her seat after giving Butter a hug. Wanting Butter to have a better view, she picked Butter up and placed her on her lap. Once they settled down, Butter looked at all that water as the boat gently moved away from the shoreline. She tried to snuggle under Debbie's arms, away from the sight of the water.

Sensing Butter's fear, Debbie coaxed, "Butter, look. Isn't it beautiful?"

"What a perfect day. The cool breeze feels good in this hot weather," Debbie noted.

Soothing stringed instruments music played Christian standards low in the background, as the captain gave a history and highlights about the Atlantic seacoast. After about five minutes into the ride, Butter finally relaxed in Debbie's lap.

Butter looked around. She lifted up on her hind feet while still in Debbie's lap, over Debbie's shoulder for a better look. She saw in the next stall a large tomcat named Ruff. Ruff saw her too.

Butter purred.

Butter was not hooked up to a post. Debbie missed the earlier instructions to keep all pets on a leash tied to a stall.

At this time a waiter came by and asked Debbie, "Would you like a beverage and sandwich?"

Debbie looked for something she wanted. While she was temporarily distracted, Butter slowly moved from Debbie's shoulder to her lap.

"Sure. What kind do you have?" She viewed the sandwich selections more closely. "I'll take the egg sandwich and orange juice."

Butter slowly crept off Debbie's lap and gently slid further away from Debbie until the leash that was in Debbie's lap slipped down to the floor.

"Would you like sausage with that, Miss?" the waiter asked.

"Only if it's vegetarian."

Butter quietly climbed the side of the railing to get over to Ruff's stall.

"We've got it right here," the waiter said as he eagerly pulled out of his rolling butler cart some hot veggie sausages.

"I'm impressed. Thanks."

Butter made it to the top of the railing. Ruff nodded

his head, coaxing her to continue. Butter's eyes focused on Ruff as she inched her way over toward his stall.

"Hot coffee or hot chocolate?"

"I'll take the hot chocolate. Thank you."

As she turned around, she looked down to the floor for Butter. By the time she looked up, there was Butter on top of the railing trying to walk over to the other stall.

"Oh no, Butter! What are you doing? Butter, come back here now!" Debbie shouted.

Butter saw Debbie and then looked down at the water. She panicked. Butter froze. She looked at the ocean below and started shaking. The cruise boat was bobbing up and down with the waves. Butter tried to force her jittery legs into the right direction, toward the deck and Debbie. She moved the front right paw toward the stall to try to get off of the rail, back into her stall.

"Are you crazy, cat? You're going to fall into the ocean if you don't come back," the waiter shouted at Butter.

Butter looked at the ocean, and gave out a weak meow.

"I'm sorry, I didn't mean to scare you. Come on, come on back this way, kitty, kitty," said the waiter.

Just as Butter tried to step off the railing toward the waiter, the boat movement swayed downward toward the ocean. The sway caused her to lose her balance as she fell on her stomach. She tried to get back on her feet onto the railing to step down, but her feet slipped again. She teetered along the outer side of the railing on her stomach, as all four legs dangled loosely.

"Don't look down," the waiter warned.

Butter looked down at the water.

Debbie and the waiter reached out to grab her.

About that time, Stewart and Bread were standing on the lower deck directly below Debbie's stall.

Stewart commented, "This view is great, Bread."

Bread agreed with a nod of his head and wave of his tail.

"Butter!" said Debbie, just inches from Butter. Butter slid down the railing on her stomach further away. She made a final attempt to reach for Debbie with her paws, but her position and movement made it futile.

In a split second, Stewart and Bread saw a cat fall from the upper deck into the Atlantic Ocean with a great splash.

Butter cried, "Meow!"

"Is that what I thought I saw?" Stewart said in disbelief.

"Couldn't be."

"Cat overboard! Cat overboard!" the waiter bellowed.

"Kill the engine!" Captain Andrew shouted.

"Butter, Butter! Somebody save Butter! Please help her. Please God, save Butter!" Debbie pleaded in desperation.

Butter was in the ocean flailing her legs about aimlessly fighting to stay afloat. Her head went under the cold water as she frantically thrashed around with her paws just enough to get her head back above the waves. She took quick breaths in her panic. She went below the surface of the water again and tried to thrash her way back up.

As she yelled, "meow" over and over, some of the water got into her mouth.

Just about this time, Captain Andrew rushed to the edge of the boat where Bread was located. He was in Stewart's stall now with a lifesaver tied to a long rope. He tossed the lifesaver into the water for Butter to grab hold, but Butter frantically gasped for breath and was unable to grab the lifesaver. She saw the lifesaver, but the ocean waves took her further away from it.

"This isn't working. We've got to think of something else," Captain Andrew said hurriedly.

"What about a lifeboat?" Stewart suggested.

"There isn't enough time. By the time we lower it, it may be too late," Captain Andrew explained.

Stewart looked at Bread and said, "You know how to swim. Jump in and get the cat."

Bread took a closer look and noticed the cat. Bread started to move toward the middle of the boat as far away as possible from the railing.

"No. Not that way, this way, Bread. Let me unhook this leash," Stewart said unhooking Bread.

"Good idea. We'll hook you to a lifesaver and rope. You can hold onto the cat while we hold onto you with the rope and lifejacket," Captain Andrew instructed Bread.

Bread continued to move away from the railing and resist getting hooked up to the lifejacket.

Stewart saw that Bread was not cooperating.

"Bread, you've got to do this. It's the Christian thing to do.

I know you're just a dog, but I'm your master."

While Stewart was having this conversation with Bread, Captain Andrew had already secured and tied a lifejacket that was attached to a long rope around Bread.

"Yes. We've got to hurry. She doesn't have much time," Captain Andrew said while helping Stewart to get Bread to jump.

Debbie yelled from the upper deck, "She's going under again. Do something. I can't lose Butter. Somebody go in there and get her or else I'll jump in myself to save her."

By this time, Abby, the resort owner's wife, had arrived at Debbie's stall and grabbed Debbie's arm.

"Don't jump. You'll only make matters worse. We're doing everything we can. It's going to work out."

"Yes. It will," Debbie meekly agreed.

"Captain Andrew knows what to do. Butter is in good hands with him. You just stay right here," Abby said, firmly holding on to Debbie's arm, just in case.

"Butter, hang in there. Someone is coming to get you. Hang on," Debbie shouted through her tears.

"Listen, Bread. You hear that? You're the only one that can rescue her," Stewart said as he picked Bread up with Captain Andrew's assistance and lifted him over the rail with the lifejacket and rope attached.

"Go get her, Bread," Captain Andrew commanded.

Bread was gently tossed into the ocean. He started swimming to Butter. Butter frantically struggled to stay afloat. Butter gasped as she saw a dog coming toward her. Butter tried to turn her back to get away from him, but since she couldn't swim, he got closer and closer. Bread was just a foot away from her now. Bread inched closer. Butter fainted. No longer fighting the waves, she went under the water again. This time she swallowed so much water that it got into her lungs.

Bread reached the spot where he saw her go under. He fought the buoyancy of the lifejacket as he dived under the water to find her. At first he didn't see her. He came up for air and dived under again, this time a little deeper, struggling with every muscle in his body. He saw her drifting downward. Bread quickly grabbed her by her collar with his teeth and allowed the lifejacket to bounce them back up to the surface.

"He's got her! He's got her!" Captain Andrew rejoiced. "Pull them in closer to the boat."

Debbie watched every minute of the rescue with Abby there to comfort and constrain her from doing anything foolish. Within a minute they were near the side of the boat. An animal rescue net waited for them just under the surface of the water. As Bread paddled with Butter still in tow, the net was positioned under them. The net was shaped like a rectangular shaped mesh net bed and reinforced on the sides with strong aluminum metal tubing.

"Pull it up. Pull it up. Gently now. There you go. We've got you in just a second," Captain Andrew calmly said.

Abby took Debbie directly to the First Aid Station. Captain Andrew rushed in with Butter in his arms.

"She's not breathing. Get me the resuscitator cup," the medic on board ordered.

Back on the deck, Stewart said "Good dog!" as he gave Bread a big hug. A crewman stood by with large white towels to help Bread dry off.

"What you did was really wonderful, Bread. Thanks. You got any dog biscuits?" Stewart asked a nearby crewman.

"Sure. Right here," the crewman chuckled as he gave

Bread a treat. Bread waved his tail as he ate his treat.

The boat rushed back to the shore in high speed. The passengers looked at the flashing lights of the Animal Ambulance waiting at the peer.

"I wonder if the cat is okay. Let's go see." Stewart walked Bread to the First Aid Station.

Bread went along with Stewart.

As they approached the First Aid Station's doorway, they could hear a woman crying.

"Keep trying, keep trying!" a teary eyed Debbie plead. Butter appeared lifeless on the stretcher. The boat medic continued to give her mouth-to-mouth resuscitation as he pressed down on her chest to get the water out of her lungs.

Stewart saw Butter motionless and remarked, "Wow. I feel sorry for Butter. I hope she's okay."

Debbie was so intensely focused on Butter's treatment that she did not notice Stewart and Bread standing at the entrance of the room. Stewart stood there speechless as he nudged Bread to come a little closer. They walked over to Butter, who was still not responding.

Stewart spoke in a low whisper, "Come on, kit. You can make it."

Miraculously, Butter started breathing and coughed up water. Her eyes opened. The first thing she saw was Bread.

She turned to her other side and saw Debbie.

"Butter. You made it! You're alive! You're going to be okay," Debbie smiled as she wiped away her tears.

"Let's get her to the hospital as soon as possible,"

Captain Andrew directed the medic. "By the way, this was the dog that jumped in to rescue Butter." He introduced Bread to Debbie.

Debbie looked up for the first time and saw Bread who was standing with Stewart. "Is this your dog?" Debbie looked at Bread and then back to Stewart.

"Yes. His name is Bread," Stewart repeated.

Debbie reached down to pat Bread on the head. "I can't thank you enough. God bless you." Then Debbie looked up at Stewart. "Aren't you the same person on the plane?" Debbie recalled.

"I believe so. What a pleasure to see you, again. The name's Stewart, Stewart Counts. And your name is?"

"Deborah Dents. Debbie is fine."

"The boat has docked, Debbie. The ambulance is waiting."

The medic took Butter and Debbie to the ambulance. Stewart and Bread left the boat with the rest of the passengers. They stood by the ambulance to see what was going on.

"Butter, there's an ambulance waiting for you. They have a doctor in the ambulance, so that you can get the best of care." Debbie comforted Butter.

Just as the ambulance door opened, out stepped Dr. Caesar.

"Hi. Where is the patient? There you are. Kind of big for a puppy, aren't you?"

"Doctor, she is a cat. This is Butter."

"Did you say Butterballs? Kind of pudgy, are you? Just kidding. Yes. I see she is a cat. What's the problem today?"

54

"She almost drowned. She's going to be all right, isn't she?"

"Let me see. Open your mouth wide. The tonsils look just fine," the doctor joked. After a quick exam of her vital signs the doctor reported, "She's fine. We'll just take her to the vet hospital for observation for an hour or two."

The ambulance was about ready to close the door. Butter stood up on the stretcher in the ambulance to see what was happening. Just before the door closed, she saw Bread standing outside with Stewart.

She looked straight at Bread and purred.

Bread waved his tail.

The ambulance door closed. The ambulance siren blared as it sped off to the vet hospital, leaving Stewart and Bread just standing there, gazing into the horizon.

Finally, after standing there on the shore for several minutes, Stewart reflected, "What a coincidence, Bread, that she was the same person I sat next to on the plane. Let's go back to the room. I think we've had enough excitement for the day."

Bread jumped around and gleefully wagged his tail.

9

After Stewart returned to his hotel room, he ordered a large lunch from the free room service.

"I wonder if that secret admirer card came from Debbie. Who else could it be? I don't know anyone here. It must have been from her. I saw her eyeing me on the plane. She was cool on the boat, just trying to hide her feelings from me. Yeah, I bet that was her that left this card. What do you think, Bread?" Bread, exhausted from the morning's event, fell asleep.

"I think I'll just read and relax for a while." Stewart reclined in an easy chair. After several minutes, he heard a knock at the door. "Who is it?" Stewart asked.

"Bellhop, sir. I have a package for you." Stewart inquisitively opened the door.

"I have a gift basket for you, sir."

"Who is this from?"

"She didn't say, sir. She just wanted me to give this to you."

"She? What did she look like?" Stewart asked.

"I don't know. The front desk clerk must have taken it, and then left it at the Bellhop's Station to deliver. It had your name on it," was all the bellhop could add.

"Thank you," a puzzled Stewart said as he closed the door. He opened the package and saw two wine glasses, a bottle of non-alcoholic wine, some cheese and crackers and mints.

The smell of the crackers woke Bread up. He went over to Stewart with the basket and inspected it further by sniffing.

"That's not for you, buddy," Stewart said to Bread.

Bread went back to his dog bed.

"How sweet of Debbie to send this thank you basket for helping Butter," Stewart reflected. "How did she know that I didn't drink?" he pondered. "Maybe I'll ask her to dinner tonight, just to thank her for the basket. Nothing else." The excitement of the day finally caught up with Stewart. He laid down on the bed to continue reading the magazine. His head nodded up and down in drowsiness.

There was a knock on the door.

"Come in."

The door opened, and it was Debbie standing there in the most provocative red spaghetti strap chiffon body-clinging dress. She was wearing 4-inch spike red high-heeled strapped sandals. One arm was up high on the edge of the doorway and the other arm was motioning Stewart to come closer. Her enticing eyes sparkled pleasure. Stewart walked over to her and took her hand leading her to the bed. Before he could say a word, she was French-kissing him and wrapping her leg around his. He fell backward onto the bed, as she moved her hands through his hair. Helplessly, he gave up all resistance.

"Bark, bark, bark! Bark, bark!"

Stewart struggled to open his eyes and saw Bread standing there, barking. "What? What? Where did she go?" Stewart looked around the room. There was no one there with him but Bread.

"Whew! What a dream. What's the barking about, Bread?"

Bread ran to the patio door. Standing outside was Butter.

Stewart looked to see if Debbie was with her. There was no Debbie in sight.

"That's odd, Bread. Why is Butter here? Let's go outside and see what's going on. But first I have to freshen up and change clothes."

Bread eagerly dashed out through the patio door to see his new friend. They jumped around the grounds playing "Hide and Seek."

Unnoticed by Bread and Butter nearby was a mysterious photographer with a telescopic lens, hiding behind a bush 50 yards away, taking pictures of their games.

Just then, Bread and Butter heard Stewart calling them.

"Bread and Butter, where are you?" Stewart had freshened up with clean clothes and cologne. He spotted them about 10 yards away. Stewart looked around for Debbie. "Where is Debbie?" Stewart asked Butter. He walked down the grassy lawn looking for her. "Come on. Let's get you back to Debbie.

She must be nearby somewhere." Stewart walked further down the back of the hotel. Stewart watched the pets play, as he looked around for Debbie. They were outside the hotel's Cat Wing.

"Come here Bread," Stewart motioned with his hands.

Bread promptly returned to Stewart, followed closely by Butter.

"I can see you're having a great time with Butter, but we've got to find Debbie. She must be worried about Butter."

Stewart and Bread followed Butter. Finally, at the back of Debbie's room, Butter jumped over the high fence to the enclosed patio off from Debbie's room. Stewart got there just in time to see Butter slip back into her hotel room. Debbie slept through Butter's entire absence.

"That must be where Debbie's room is," Stewart said as he counted the number of patio doors down from the entrance of the hotel. "Her room was three doors down from the entrance. Bread, let's go see if she's okay."

During this same time, Ralph was staking out the grounds.

He had perched himself up in a tree on the hotel grounds, watching the whole thing between Bread and Butter and Stewart, through his large binoculars.

"Finding Debbie is going to be easier than I thought," Ralph whispered to himself.

"Let's go inside, Bread, to check on Debbie," Stewart told Bread.

Bread eagerly followed Stewart into the hotel lobby and down the Cat Wing corridor of the hotel.

"Excuse me, sir. Where is Bread's leash?" Timothy inquired, filling in for Martha at the front desk.

"I left it in the room," a momentarily distracted Stewart replied.

"No problem. We have spare ones right here. What kind do you like?"

Stewart hurriedly went over to the desk to pick out a leash.

"We have green, yellow, blue and..." Timothy offered Stewart.

"I'll take any color." Stewart said quickly. "What size do you want? A ½ inch, 1 inch or..." Timothy continued.

"Doesn't matter," Stewart answered in frustration.

While Stewart was still trying to get out of the lobby to see Debbie, Ralph tried as quietly and inconspicuously as possible to go through the lobby to the Cat Wing side. He counted three doors down to Room C-3. He stood there, one fist posed to knock on the door. He took a deep breath and looked down to the floor. Around his neck were foot long binoculars. Plus, his pants had a big dirt spot on them from climbing in the tree. Even his shoes were muddy from the water sprinkler system on the lawn. "I'd better come back later," Ralph decided.

"And the style? We have traditional and contemporary," Timothy continued explaining to Stewart.

"I don't care! Just give me any leash," an annoyed Stewart said.

"Now this is very stylish, but kind of trendy. What do you think?" Timothy said. Without saying another word Stewart grabbed a leash from Timothy.

"I'll take this one. How much?" Stewart asked, trying to wrap this transaction up quickly.

"No charge for the first one. Just give us your room number, please."

"D-5," Stewart yelled as he rushed over to the entrance to the Cat Wing.

Ralph, who was dashing out of the Cat Wing, but looking down trying to wipe some of the dirt off of his pants with his hands, brushed up against Stewart by accident.

"Excuse me," Stewart said apologetically, barely noticing Ralph.

Ralph didn't respond. He discreetly stood by a room several doors down, pretending to open a door. He turned his head away from Debbie's door as he attempted to eavesdrop.

"I think this is the room Butter went into from the outside."

Stewart counted down three doors from the inside hallway of the hotel.

"Knock, knock." There was no answer. "Knock, knock, knock."

Bread started barking, "bark, bark, bark."

Butter meowed back.

Bread started barking again, and Butter started meowing, until it sounded like they were in a duet. Before you knew it, the other cats in the nearby rooms were singing in chorus with Bread and Butter.

Debbie, with all the noise, finally woke up. Still sleepy-eyed, she got up from the bed and went to the door to see what all the noise was about. She looked through the peephole and saw Stewart standing outside of her door.

"What are you doing here?" Debbie asked in surprise.

"I came to return your cat, Butter."

Debbie looked down at her feet and there was Butter, rubbing up against her ankles purring.

"Butter is right here with me. I wasn't expecting company," Debbie said, still confused.

"Butter must have slipped back into your room from the patio door. I can explain. While I'm here can you open the door?"

Debbie looked over to the patio door and saw that the pet door was ajar.

"It looks like Butter probably did slip out and return." She gave Butter a stern look. Butter purred innocently.

"Stewart, I don't allow men into my hotel room," a straight-faced Debbie informed him.

Stewart bent down and whispered to Bread, "The least she could do is open the door. Who does she think I am? A dog?"

"No offense, Bread." He regrouped.

"Sure. I can respect that. Can we meet at the hotel restaurant and have dinner tonight?"

Debbie smiled, "Thank you for your respect. Okay to dinner."

Stewart, looking down at Bread added, "Let's leave our pets in their rooms."

"I don't know. I read in the welcome booklet that they have pet sitters. I'll see if I can find out the details," Debbie said, "I am kind of reluctant to leave Butter alone."

"Sounds great. See you at seven?"

"Fine. See you at seven."

Ralph, having heard all he needed, stopped pretending to get in a stranger's room and swiftly left the Cat Wing.

Debbie looked at Butter and said, "You won't mind, would you, Butter? I think they have a Pet Care Center.

You'll get to meet some other cats to play with."

As Stewart began walking back to his room he told Bread, "I hear they have the best gourmet dog biscuits in Savannah at the Pet Care Center." Stewart reassuringly patted Bread on the head.

Wagging his tail and jumping up and down, Bread barked with excitement.

Stewart and Bread proceeded back to their room in the Dog Wing, to get ready for dinner.

"Go look at the pet channel while I take a shower, Bread. I'll be out in a jiffy."

Stewart's phone rang.

"Hello," Stewart answered the phone.

"Hello, Mr. Counts. You have a message at the front desk."

"Who is it from?" a puzzled Stewart asked.

"There's no name, sir. Shall I read it to you?"

"Yes, please do."

"I'll meet you in the dining room at 6:30 p.m. tonight. I'll be wearing red."

"That's odd, I thought she said seven?"

"Anything else?"

"No, sir."

"Thanks for the message."

"You're welcome."

10

"What do you think, Butter?" Debbie asked Butter. "Is this dress okay? I really hadn't planned on going on a date during this vacation."

Butter looked at the sleeveless red summer silk blouse with the mock turtleneck collar and matching long sleeve ¾ length jacket and loose fitting, but tapered, red silk pants.

"I think these pearl earrings and necklace will work with the white shoes and purse. What do you think, huh, Butter?" Debbie asked, knowing that Butter didn't know what she was talking about.

"I better take that shower now. I've got to get ready and take you to the Pet Care Center before my 7:00 p.m. date," Debbie reasoned. Having second thoughts about going on a date with someone she just met, Debbie sat in the chair and continued talking to Butter.

"Stewart seemed nice, but you can't trust men. All they want to do is get you in bed."

Butter climbed on Debbie's lap to comfort her and purred.

Debbie's attention moved to looking at the Bible. As her eyes followed Butter and then saw the Bible, she prayed, "Lord, if you could just guide me, show me your way." She sat there for a moment to hear from the Lord. She reached for the Bible and flipped it open and read Proverbs 3:5-6: *Trust in the Lord...and He shall direct thy path.* "Dear Lord, guide me. Give me wisdom,

Amen. Wow, look at the clock. I'd better get moving." She rushed to the bathroom to take a shower.

Stewart arrived at the Pet Care Center with Bread. "Hi. I made reservations for my pet to be with the sitter tonight. This is Bread." Stewart introduced him to the pet sitter.

"Yes. Hello, Stewart. What a nice dog you have. I'm sure he will enjoy his evening with us. Any special requests?" asked the high school student, Mike, the pet sitter for the Pet Care Center that evening.

"Give him the best biscuits you've got and he'll be okay."

"We can do that."

"Bye, Bread. See you later tonight."

Bread was focused on food and eagerly went with Mike. He was one of the first pets there for the evening. Things were pretty quiet. A few more pets arrived, but they were shy, making for a very peaceful time.

A little while later, Debbie brought Butter to the Pet Care Center.

"Take good care of Butter. She is sweet and I know you will be gentle with her. She's had a rough day and probably just wants to relax."

"Most definitely, Debbie. You can rest assured that she is in safe hands with us," Mike assured her.

Debbie gave one last hug to Butter. "I forgot my purse. I need to go back to my room to get it." She rushed back to her room before meeting Stewart for dinner.

Debbie got back to her room and grabbed her purse.

Her phone rang.

"Hello."

"Hi, Will," Debbie replied.

"How's it going, Sis?"

"Don't ask. Other than Butter almost drowning this morning, fine."

"Meet anybody yet?"

"As a matter of fact, I did. He's from Detroit. I'm meeting him for dinner tonight."

"That soon?"

"I thought you said have fun and meet someone?"

"Yeah, go right ahead. What's his name?"

"Stewart."

"What does he do for a living?"

"I have no idea. Whatever it is, it doesn't pay much."

"Why do you say that?"

"On the plane, he didn't know that the snacks were free, so he doesn't travel much. The way he dresses makes me think he's just getting by. I don't know how he could afford a vacation like this."

"Money's not everything, Sis."

"He doesn't have to be rich, but I at least want someone that has a stable source of income."

"You're not getting serious with him anyway, right?"

"Right."

"He's just someone to occupy your time while you're on vacation for a week. When you come back to Detroit, you won't have to worry about his income," Will protectively concluded.

"Right again."

Stewart arrived at the restaurant promptly at 6:30 p.m.

"I have reservations for two, under 'Counts.'"

"Right this way, Mr. Counts. And your other person's name?" the maitre d' asked.

"She'll know who I am," Stewart smiled.

"I'll escort her to your table as soon as she arrives. Here is the dinner menu. My name is Girard, your maitre d' for the evening."

"Thank you."

While waiting for Debbie, Stewart went straight to the prices on the menu. He mumbled, "Boy, these prices are high. There must be something on the low end."

Less than a minute later, Gloria walked into the restaurant.

"May I help you, madam?" Girard asked.

"Yes. I'm meeting someone here. There he is." Gloria pointed to Stewart's table. She was wearing a skimpy, red chemise mini-dress with spaghetti straps. The outfit barely covered her body. Her red four-inch spike heel shoes matched her red purse and bright red lipstick. Her long auburn hair flowed down her back and her perfume was sweet and sensual. She had a touch of glitter in her hair. Her skin glowed from a special lotion with sparkles. Her eyes were illuminated from the sparkling eye shadow.

Stewart was still engrossed in the large menu selection.

He didn't notice that anyone was approaching his table.

"Will this seat be okay for you, Miss Harps?"

"Yes. This is fine, thank you, Girard."

Stewart looked up from the menu smiling. His smile quickly turned to a frown when he saw Gloria, his secretary. "Gloria?

What? How? Is that you Gloria? Of course it is. I thought you were in Detroit."

"Yes. It's me," Gloria said calmly.

"What a surprise." Stewart said, nearly speechless.

"That makes two of us. Imagine you and I picking the same resort? Go figure," Gloria said coyly.

Stewart just sat there in shock.

Gloria continued, "I figured that since the boss was on vacation for a week, this would be a good time for me to take a vacation. What looks good, besides me?" Gloria lowered her head to study the menu.

"You didn't tell me you were going on vacation."

"You weren't there to ask. Besides, after the big deal closed, I didn't have anything else to do."

"How could you afford a vacation like this?"

"Your boss gave me a bonus too. I don't want to spend my vacation talking about the job. What do you recommend from the menu? Everything looks delicious." Gloria looked Stewart up and down with her eyes.

Still in shock, Stewart managed to say, "How did we end up at the same hotel? I get it. You got the information from the travel agent, Sharon, didn't you?"

"I did send you to the travel agent who happens to be my best friend."

"I don't believe this." Stewart tapped the palm of his

hand to his forehead in disgust.

"I've spent all day getting ready for this evening, not to mention the trip and money it cost me to get here. Say something. Say, 'you look beautiful, Gloria. I'm so glad to see you.'"

"You look nice, Gloria. I hope you enjoy your dinner, but I'm expecting someone."

"I don't mind. He can join us at the table. I might have known you'd find some business to discuss. We can all sit together."

"Gloria, he, I mean she, is a woman. I don't think that would be such a good idea. It's not a business meeting."

"I see." She put the menu down on the table. She looked around the room and noticed Ralph. She took a deep breath and exhaled, "I've got a date too. I was just coming over to say hello."

"You do? Great."

She took another deep breath, got up and approached Ralph.

She leaned over to Ralph's ear, with her back facing Stewart, and whispered in Ralph's ear, "Let's *pretend* you're my date.

I'm trying to impress that guy over there," as she motioned her eyes in the direction of Stewart's table.

Ralph took one look, a second and a third at Gloria's cleavage, waist and rear end and said, "Sure babe. After dinner, let's *pretend* to go back to my room and *pretend* to get it on."

"You're disgusting. I wouldn't go to bed with you if you paid me a million dollars."

70

"How about two?" Ralph chided.

"Shut up and order from the menu. I've got to make this look good."

Stewart looked at his watch and saw that it was ten minutes after seven. While sitting there he mumbled, "That anonymous note, gift basket and message must have been from Gloria, not Debbie. I wonder if Debbie is going to show up. Maybe she was just being polite." He nervously looked at his watch again. It was now fifteen after seven. He motioned Girard over to his table. "I must have gotten the time wrong. I guess I'll wait just a few more minutes, then return to my hotel room."

"I'm just checking on you to make sure you're okay," Will said, still on the phone with Debbie.

"Butter and I are fine. I've got to go. Look at the clock. I'm late. It's fifteen after seven already. Talk to you later."

"Love ya, Sis."

"Love you too, Will."

Ralph explained to Gloria, "Look, sug, I'm a little tied up right now. I'm expecting a lady friend."

"You too?" a disappointed Gloria said.

Debbie arrived at the restaurant. Stewart had walked almost to the entrance when he saw Debbie arrive.

Just then, Ralph saw Debbie approach Stewart, so he grabbed Gloria's arm quickly, just as she stood up to leave.

"On second thought, I'd rather be with you. Is the name Gloria? See. I remembered your name."

"Hi Debbie. You made it." Stewart walked Debbie back to his table. He pulled the chair out for her to sit.

"Hi Stewart. Thank you."

Gloria's back was turned to Stewart's table and therefore she didn't see Debbie's arrival.

"Sorry, I'm late. I had a phone call just as I was leaving the room."

"No problem. A boyfriend?" Stewart inquired.

"No. It was my brother, checking up on me."

"He's not planning any surprise trips down here?"

"No," Debbie laughed. "He knows I can take care of myself."

Stewart changed the subject, "I see you're wearing red. That must be a very popular color around here."

"It's my favorite color. What's yours?"

"Grey or blue. I mean I really haven't thought about it.

Whatever costs the least," Stewart laughed.

"Oh."

"Hey maitre d'." Ralph motioned Girard to come to his table.

"Got any drinks?" Ralph bluntly asked.

"Good evening. I'm Girard, your maitre d' for the evening.

Yes, sir. We have coffee, tea and juice."

"I mean liquor, the hard stuff. You know."

"No sir. This is a family restaurant. Our owner, David Shepherd, does not allow that."

"How about beer?"

"No sir."

"Wine?"

"Absolutely not, sir. Alcohol would be bad for the animals. Mr. Shepherd doesn't want it around them, sir."

"Do I look like an animal? You must have something?"

"Not really."

"Let me think for a minute." Ralph placed his hand to his chin.

"That's a switch," Gloria snickered.

"Got grape juice?"

"It's not on the menu, but I can see if we have some grape juice."

"What is this, a convent? Just put it in a couple of wine glasses. I've got an image to maintain."

"Will water goblets be okay, sir?"

"Yeah, yeah. Make that on the rocks and make it quick.

Looking at this chick is making me thirsty."

The maitre d' went off to get the juice.

"I kind of like this pet hotel thing. Tell me something, babe.

Want to be my pet so we can pet?"

Gloria looked furious as she clinched her lips and squinted her eyes at Ralph, like a teacher ready to give a stern lecture.

"Just kidding." He backed off.

A few minutes later, Girard returned to Stewart's table.

"What would you like to order, madam?" the maitre d' asked Debbie.

"Order whatever you like," Stewart said, who barely got the words out of his mouth after looking at the prices on the menu.

"I'll get a vegetarian plate. I see they have quite a selection.

I'll take the bean cakes and sweet potato soufflé. How about you, Stewart?"

"Just water, thank you. I'm really not hungry."

Girard turned to Stewart.

"Are you sure? We have several specials tonight. Plus there is a world renowned gourmet chef visiting with us who can prepare just about anything you like."

Stewart looked at the menu again.

"Got any breadsticks?"

Both Debbie and the maitre d' looked at him strangely.

"Yes, sir. I'll bring you an assortment." The maitre d' collected the menus and walked away.

"Ever been to Savannah before?" Debbie asked.

"No. Have you?"

"No. I plan to come back. It's really beautiful down here," Debbie chatted.

"Here is your salad," the maitre d' said, as he carefully placed the plate of mixed greens in front of Debbie. He plopped down Stewart's plate of breadsticks with a heavy thud, as he looked straight at Stewart.

"Would you like any fresh ground pepper on your salad, madam?"

"Yes, please."

"And you sir? Would you like any pepper on your... breadsticks?"

"No!" Stewart said, annoyed.

Girard returned to Ralph's table.

"Doll, with that cute figure, don't order anything fattening,"

"I'll order what I like, because you don't have to worry about my figure," Gloria scolded.

"I'll come back to your table after you two lovebirds make up your minds," Girard said.

11

"Here are your dinners. Watch the plates, they are hot," Girard warned Debbie and Stewart.

Stewart touched his plate, which was filled with breadsticks.

"Ouch!" He looked up at the maitre d' in disgust.

"I told you it was hot," Girard smirked at Stewart. He had pre-heated a plate of breadsticks.

Debbie looked at her vegetarian plate and smelled the wonderful aroma of herbs and spices from the bean cakes and sweet potato soufflé.

"Hmm. Looks great," she complimented Girard.

"Thank you. Enjoy your meals." Girard walked away.

A photographer in a masked costume came to the table, smiled and snapped pictures. She mysteriously walked away, just as quickly without saying a word.

"That was a very nice camera the hotel photographer had.

I especially liked the zoom lens," Debbie observed.

"You know something about cameras?" Stewart asked.

"A little. It's my hobby. I got into it while taking 'before and after' pictures of my interior design work."

"You're an interior designer? Do you like what you

do?"

"Very much so. I like the freedom to express myself while also making other people's dreams come true. Do you have any hobbies?"

"If you want to call it a hobby, I like to cook gourmet meals. It's relaxing after a high intensity day in the real estate business."

"You're in real estate? What kind?"

"Commercial real estate law. I'm an attorney and real estate sales agent."

"That's interesting. Did your work bring you to Savannah?"

Debbie inquired, caught off guard by the difference between his profession and his appearance.

"Yes and no. I've been working so hard that I didn't have time to spend with Bread, my dog. I thought this would be a great way to relax and have some quality time with him."

"Would you believe, that's the same reason I came here. I wanted to get away while I'm in between projects, to enjoy the week with my cat, Butter."

"We've got something in common, already," Stewart smiled.

"That was thoughtful of you to bring your pet on your vacation," Debbie smiled back.

"What else do you like to do with the little spare time that you have?" Stewart asked.

"I recently started a group called 'SafeCity,' which is a small group of women who get together to explore non-violent ways to root out violence in our society."

"That shouldn't be too hard. Just pull out the stray

roots," Stewart joked while chopping on his breadsticks, which made a lot of noise.

"And you've got a sense of humor too," Debbie laughed.

Girard returned to their table. "I can hear you eating clear across the room, sir. Could you tone the chomping down, just a little?"

Stewart gave him an embarrassed, but irritated look.

"Are you enjoying your meal, Ms. Dents?" Girard politely asked Debbie.

"Yes. These bean cakes are delicious."

"What kind of breadsticks are these?" Stewart asked Girard.

"Extra, extra crispy," Girard said with a half grin, then walked away.

"I don't think I should give our maitre d' a tip," Stewart conjectured.

Debbie changed the subject. She was feeling more relaxed.

"Do you have a girlfriend or wife?"

Stewart looked at Debbie and clumsily stammered out, "Well, no. I don't have either." He tried to clear his dry throat. In response, he nervously reached for his glass of water a little too fast, knocking it over on the table.

"My dress!" Debbie shouted and stood up immediately to avoid additional water flowing her way, some of which had spilled on her lap.

"I'm so sorry I spilled the water on you. Let me wipe it off."

Stewart quickly reached for the front of Debbie's

dress with his napkin.

Debbie jumped up and away, "That won't be necessary. I'll just dry it off in the restroom. I'll be right back."

Ralph had been watching Debbie out of the corner of his eye and decided to make his move.

"I'll be right back, toots, gotta take a leak," Ralph said to Gloria.

"Don't hurry back."

Ralph followed Debbie to the restroom.

"Excuse me. Which way to the men's room? Why, is that you, Debbie? What are you doing here?" Ralph faked surprise.

Debbie looked up and saw Ralph.

"Ralph? What are you doing here?"

"I have a gig down here. What a pleasant surprise."

"I don't believe you. What gig?" Debbie suspiciously drilled him.

"Here at the hotel. They are letting me stay here while I play for them. What a coincidence, huh?"

"How did you know I was here? Did you follow me?"

"Of course not, Debbie."

"Stay away from me, Ralph, or you will get what you got in Detroit."

Ralph backed away by a few feet, but continued talking.

"What happened to your dress?"

"None of you business." Debbie disappeared in a

huff into the ladies' room.

Ralph mumbled, "That's a start. We're talking." He returned to his table where Gloria was sitting.

"So, Gloria, what brings you here to this hotel? Don't tell me to spend quality time with your goldfish."

Gloria glanced over to Stewart's table, which was partially hidden behind a large green-leaf plant and said, "That guy over there is my boss. I'm his secretary. I'm crazy about him.

I'm hoping I can get him to notice me during this trip, so we'll be dating before we go back to Detroit."

"How interesting. I happen to stay in the same apartment building as the lady he is sitting with. We've got a thing going on. I came here to take the relationship to a higher level, if you know what I mean."

"You mean lower level."

"That's not a bad idea, although I never thought of that."

"Figures. What I want to know is how does your friend and my boss know each other?"

"What makes you think that they met before?"

"I really don't know that. Maybe they did just meet."

"It's my guess that they just met, because Debbie doesn't date anyone for long."

"Why is that?"

"You might say that she has a certain knee-jerk reaction when men get too close to her. But I'm going to change that."

"It's probably just when you come around her," Gloria laughed.

Ignoring Gloria's remark, Ralph questioned, "Now, that fella she's with, I don't know anything about him."

"I do. Stewart's cheap, works 24/7 and is rich. I'm surprised that he doesn't have his laptop with him."

"Rich? How rich?"

"Millions. But I'm not interested in his money."

"Sure. Tell me anything. Let me guess, you came down here on a secretary's salary just to be near him."

"Right."

"Winning Debbie over to be with me is going to be tougher than I thought."

"Hold that thought. I've got to go to the ladies' room."

Debbie had returned from the restroom and her dress was dry. But she was still upset over seeing Ralph. Now she was acting nervous. She started fidgeting with her fork and knife. She absently picked up the knife and wrapped her hand around it in a tight fist. She tried to restart the conversation, even though she was still angry at Ralph.

"Tell me about dogs, I mean, your pet dog, Bread," Debbie said, still thinking about Ralph.

"Bread is my best friend. We do as much as we can together."

"That's nice," Debbie said absently, not sure of what Stewart had just said.

"Do you know anyone in Savannah?" Stewart asked, noticing her sudden uneasiness. The thought of just seeing Ralph and hearing that question made her muscles tense up even further.

Just as she said, "No, I don't," in a slightly elevated

tone of voice, she flung her hand that held the knife in an upward swinging motion and before she knew it, she knocked over her water glass with the knife still in her hand, causing the water to spill into Stewart's lap. In a panic, she quickly stood up with the knife in her hand. Stewart froze at the sight of her standing there, with her fist still clinched around the knife. Realizing how this looked, she dropped it immediately on the table causing a loud thump.

"I'm so sorry. Did any of the water get on you?" she asked in a daze.

They both looked down and Stewart was drenched with the water all over the front of his pants, causing a large noticeably dark stain.

"Just a little. I'll be right back." He rushed to the restroom and ran into Gloria who was on her way out of the lady's restroom.

"You could have at least waited until you got into the hotel room," she said gazing down at his wet pants.

"It's not what you think, Gloria. Besides, I'm having a great evening, sort of."

"Whatever you say, boss."

Stewart disappeared into the restroom to dry his pants.

12

"I'm ready for the bill now," Stewart said to Girard.

"Your room number, sir?"

"I'm not charging this to my room. I'm paying cash, so can you just please bring the bill?"

"Are you a guest here?"

"Of course. What does that have to do with anything? Just bring me the bill!" an impatient Stewart yelled through gritted teeth.

"Sir, didn't they tell you?"

"Tell me what!"

"The meals are free as part of the package for all hotel guests. All we need is your room number to verify that you are a guest.

There was no charge for the lady's dinner and your ...breadsticks," Girard grinned.

By now Debbie, almost cracking up, brought the napkin up to her mouth to hide her laughter.

"D-5," Stewart sheepishly said.

"Thank you sir, come back again, although I can't promise you our famous guest chef will be back this week." Girard turned around quickly to conceal his delight.

"Would you like to take a stroll outside?" Stewart said, trying to prolong the evening and air out his damp pants.

"It's getting late. I'd better get Butter now. She's probably tired." Debbie was still trying to get away from Ralph as soon as possible.

"Yes. Good idea. It is late. I've got to get Bread, too. Let's go get them now, together."

"Sure."

Gloria watched Debbie and Stewart leave the restaurant.

"Nice knowing you, Ralph, was it?"

"Can I call you? What's your number? I need it for the maitre d' to clear the account."

"It's C-4, but don't think about dropping by."

"And your room number?" said the maitre d', to verify that they were hotel guests.

"I'm in D-4." Ralph said loudly in earshot of Gloria.

"Call me tonight, babe," Ralph continued to yell.

"Don't hold your breath. Bye." Gloria exited the room.

Debbie and Stewart arrived at the Pet Care Center.

"Hi, Mike. We've come to pick up our pets, Bread and Butter."

"Yes ma'am and sir. I'll get them for you in a jiffy."

While standing there, Debbie couldn't help but notice how clean and neat the place was. Mike brought Butter first.

"So what are you doing Tuesday?"

"I haven't decided. Good night," Debbie repeated, trying to end the conversation.

"Good night," a dejected Stewart responded.

Stewart talked to Bread as they walked back to his room.

"We really blew that date, didn't we, Bread?"

Debbie was looking for the keycard to her hotel room when Ralph approached her from down the hallway waving his arms until he got her attention.

"Hi Debbie. There was something else I wanted to say to you tonight. You look great in that red dress. Since we're staying at the same hotel, can we maybe just see each other a little?"

Ralph walked closer to Debbie with his arms outstretched.

"Don't you come any closer," Debbie warned.

Ralph kept walking to her while talking, "Debbie I just want to..."

Before he could get his words out of his mouth, Debbie made a karate move on him. She kicked him in the groin and flipped him on the floor with her arms.

While he was groaning on the floor, she opened her door and said, "Keep it up and I won't be so nice next time."

"Debbie, I just wanted to..." Ralph moaned on the hallway floor with an outstretched hand.

Slam! went Debbie's door in his face.

"...do lunch?" Ralph asked to the closed door. He slowly got up, dusted himself off and limped away with a smile on his face mumbling, "She likes me. She really likes me. I think."

When Ralph got back to his room, the parakeet said "Jerk, Jerk."

"Oh shut up," Ralph said back to the parakeet.

"Jerk, shut up. Jerk, shut up," went the parakeet.

Ralph covered the cage and turned out the light, just before he collapsed on the bed.

Gloria retired to her room. She checked on her two goldfish, who were swimming around seeming to be having a great time. She sat on the side of the bed staring into the fishbowl.

"Before this week is over, I'm going to get my man and we will be like two fish in a fishbowl, inseparable."

Debbie, ready for bed, turned out the lights, but she couldn't sleep. She kept thinking about not only Ralph, but also the terrible impression she must have given to Stewart. She wasn't afraid of Ralph, but she was annoyed with him. "The nerve of that Ralph coming all the way to Savannah to see me. When is he going to learn that my 'no' means 'no'?" a frustrated Debbie asked Butter.

Butter, totally exhausted from the day's activities was practically snoring. Debbie turned to the passage that read Psalm 55:22: "'Cast your burden upon the Lord and he shall sustain thee.' Butter, we have had enough excitement for today. Let's get some rest."

13

Stewart checked the hotel's Tuesday itinerary, especially the "free" activities. "Look what we have scheduled today, Bread. It's a bus tour of the city. Let's get going. We want to get some good seats on the bus." Stewart jumped out of bed. After he showered, dressed and ate his pre-ordered breakfast, he took Bread for a walk. "I'm still feeling bad about the dinner last night. Maybe I'll see her on the bus tour and we can get to know each other better. What do you think, Bread?"

Bread waved his tail.

Debbie was also preparing to go on the bus tour. "Stewart must think I am a cold and aloof person the way I ended the date so fast. I sure hope I get to see him today to show him I can be warm and friendly. Think that's a good idea?" Debbie asked Butter.

Butter purred.

Stewart arrived at the bus first.

"Good morning, Mr. Counts and Mr. Bread. Your reserved seats are on the lower deck, seat 24A and B, where the larger animals are," Abby pointed to the bus' seats up front.

"Thanks. Does this mean that the cats can't sit with the dogs?" Stewart asked, a little disappointed.

"That's correct," Abby replied. "We don't want more distractions than they already have. We want all the animals to enjoy the sights and sounds of the tour."

Stewart looked out the window and saw Debbie walking to the bus. He whispered to Bread, "I'm so embarrassed about last night. Maybe I should forget about her. I guess it is just as well that we are not sitting together."

Bread nudged Stewart's hand.

"Good morning, Ms. Dents, your reserved seats are on the upper deck. They are seat numbers 15A and B. How are you feeling this morning, Miss Butter?" Abby patted Butter on the head.

Butter meowed.

Ralph and Gloria found themselves standing in line next to each other to board the bus.

"Look at this. My reserved seat is on the upper level of the bus with the cats," Gloria lamented. "I wanted to sit next to Stewart."

"I know what you mean," Ralph chimed. "I had my heart set on sitting next to Debbie. But my ticket is for the lower level deck with the dogs."

"That's probably where you belong," Gloria laughed.

"Ruff, ruff," Ralph howled.

Gloria raised her eyebrows and shook her head at him.

"What? I can't help my animal instincts. Besides, the ladies like macho."

"In what millennium?" Gloria countered. Then she suggested, "Why don't we alter the tickets like you did on the plane?"

"Because, kiddo, they know who we are, by name and by our pets. It will never work."

"We've got to think of something. I'm not giving up

that easily. We can't let them get off the bus and start talking to each other again."

"It's a free country. I don't know how you can stop them, sweetheart. What are you going to do? Lock them up? I got it, tell them that we forbid that they speak to each other," Ralph laughed.

"Very funny. I have a better idea."

"What's that?" Ralph curiously asked.

"There is only one thing we can do. We've got to make them hate each other."

"What good does that do? They'd just hate each other and us."

"No. When they stop talking to each other, we move in," Gloria explained.

"Move in? I like the sound of that."

"Pay attention," Gloria refocused Ralph.

"Sure, doll."

"Just follow my plan and you'll get your woman and I'll get my man."

"Now you've got my attention, toots."

"I know a lot about Stewart and you know a lot about Debbie. I'll tell Debbie what Stewart likes, only it will be what he hates. You can do the same with Stewart. So when they do see and speak to each other, they will be totally turned off."

"Let me get this straight, buttercup. Are you saying that I should be dishonest and give bad advice to the man? I don't know. Us guys try to stick together when it comes to how to get chicks."

"You are not catching 'chicks.'"

"We are just working a scheme so that the right person gets with the right person. We know what is best for everyone. The end justifies the means, don't you think?" Gloria reasoned with ambivalence.

"When you put it like that, darling, I guess it's okay, I think. If making Stewart look bad makes me look good, let's go for it."

"Great. We'll straighten this out in no time so that we can enjoy the rest of the trip," Gloria concluded.

"Good Morning, Ms. Harps. I see your Goldies are swimmingly well today. Please take you seats at 16A and B." Abby pointed to Gloria's seats at the upper level.

"Thank you," Gloria acknowledged.

"You may be the last, but not the least, Mr. Rolls. Good morning to you too, Talker. Please take seats at 25 A and B, lower level," Abby pointed to Ralph's seat.

"Good morning, I'm Sonny, your tour guide for today. Welcome to our double-decker bus. Sit back and relax while we take you to see the sights of Savannah, the place where your smile meets the rising sun," Sonny cheerfully recited. Gloria sat next to Debbie. Ralph sat down next to Stewart.

"Hi. My name is Ralph. What's yours?"

"Stewart. Nice to meet you."

"Nice dog you've got. What's his name?"

"Bread. What's your parakeet's name?"

"Talker as in, 'talks-too-much.'"

"That's an unusual name. What does he say?"

The parakeet piped out, "You're a jerk."

Ralph quickly scolded, "Shut up jerk, or I'll drop you off at the next bus stop."

"You're a jerk. Shut up," the parakeet repeated.

"He has a bad mouth. I don't know where he gets it," Ralph explained to Stewart.

"You meet any chicks down here?" Ralph asked, changing the subject.

"Not really. I just met one lady that I had dinner with and that was a disaster."

"That's too bad. There are plenty more out there. You shouldn't have any trouble meeting chicks."

"I don't know about that. I haven't dated much."

"Surely you've had a lot of women. How many?" Ralph dug.

"That's a little personal," Stewart defensively replied.

"You can tell me. I won't tell anyone. 100? 50? 25? 10?

How many?" Ralph probed.

"That's none of your business. Besides, guys don't tell," Stewart resisted.

"What planet are you from? Guys always tell. It's a macho thing," Ralph corrected Stewart.

"You haven't had any? Huh?" Ralph nudged.

"Shush. Don't say that so loud," Stewart confessed.

"Really? You're a virgin? I never met a grown male virgin.

Don't worry. Your secret is safe with me. Why are you a virgin, man?"

"I said lower your voice," Stewart squirmed in a whisper.

Ralph whispered back as he leaned into Stewart,

"Why, man?"

"I'm saving myself," Stewart quietly and quickly blurted out.

"For what? You don't have to worry about using it all up. It replenishes itself."

"I'm a Christian and I'm saving myself for marriage"

"Man, Christians do it. It's in the Bible, so I hear. Besides, when you go to a clothing store, don't you try on the merchandise first?"

"Women are not merchandise. Besides, come to think of it, I don't know when I've been shopping for clothes either."

Ralph sized up the outdated t-shirt and pants Stewart was wearing. "I can tell."

"What is that supposed to mean?" Stewart resentfully asked.

"Don't change the subject. We were talking about getting to know a woman in the biblical way before you commit to the forever stuff."

"I want God to choose for me because I want my marriage to last. But the whole issue is moot. I don't have time to date anyway."

"So what were you doing last night, bud?"

"I don't think it went over so well. After I spilled the water on her dress and she came back from the restroom, she was in a hurry to go."

"That's a good one, pretending to accidentally spill water on the lady's dress, so you could..."

"It was an accident. I didn't, oh why am I telling you this? She's the one that was upset because I messed up."

"Anyway, even if you don't want to 'cross the finish line,' there's no harm in going around the track a few times, just so you won't be too far behind when God says, 'Go.'"

"What's your point?"

"I have lots of experience about these things. I can get any chick I want, any time. Is she on the bus?"

"Yes. She is on the upper level," Stewart quietly said.

"When we get off the bus for a tourist stop, this is what I want you to do. When you see, what's her name?"

"Debbie."

"When you see Debbie, just come up behind her and put both of your hands on her shoulders. Chicks like for men to come up behind them and surprise them. They think it is so considerate and thoughtful. Try it," Ralph confidently advised.

"I don't know."

"You can't do much worse than last night. I mean you really blew it, right? Trust me. She'll love it," Ralph coaxed.

"Okay. What do I have to lose?"

On the lower level of the bus, Gloria was striking up a conversation with Debbie.

"Hi, I'm Gloria," Gloria cheerfully smiled at Debbie. "What's your name, may I ask?"

"Debbie."

"Nice to meet you. This is such a wonderful vacation with the pets. Only thing missing is guys," Gloria led.

"Men can be such a pain," Debbie said, thinking of her experience with Ralph last night.

"I know what you mean. But face it. There's no substitute," Gloria said.

"Then I'll just do without, thank you," Debbie resolutely said.

"Didn't I see you with someone last night?" Gloria asked.

"How did you know I was with someone last night?"

"I was on a date of my own and happened to notice you two. What do you think of him?"

"He was nice. I don't think I made a very good impression. Even if I did like him, I didn't come here to date. I came to spend time with Butter."

"Did you know that I'm an expert when it comes to men? Take what's his name."

"Stewart."

"I could size Stewart up real quick. He's not my type. But if you want to spend some more time with him, I know what that kind of man likes."

"You do? What is that?" Debbie's asked out of curiosity.

"Sex," Gloria put it succinctly.

"That leaves me out. No way, before I get married."

Trying to regroup, Gloria expounded, "No. Not *doing it* girlfriend. I mean *flaunting it*. As in looking sexy, smelling sexy and most of all, talking sexy. Yeah, guys respect that kind of woman," Gloria advised.

"Do you really think so? That's a surprise."

Gloria looked at Debbie's outfit, covered from neck to ankle, even in the hot summer sun of Savannah. "Why don't you try wearing a little different outfit, something sexy? Guys like women who dress sexy."

Debbie looked at Gloria and then herself. By comparison to Gloria, she did look a little dowdy. "I didn't bring anything sexy on the trip. I don't think I would be comfortable wearing what you are wearing; no offense."

"Listen girlfriend, it's not about comfort. It's about the catch. Do you want to spend the rest of this vacation wondering what might have been? Trust me. You can't miss with this kind of outfit. There are some stores at the next stop." Gloria pointed up ahead. "We can fix you up real quick, before the bus returns. You'll also need to know about a few lines that guys love to hear."

"What's that?"

"Men like to feel important by giving us women some money. Ask this Stewart guy for $1,000."

"I just met him. I couldn't do that. Besides, he looks so poor."

"Looks are deceiving, Debbie. Tell him you need the money to save the whales."

"I live in Detroit. There are no whales in the Detroit River. That's so far fetched."

"Then make up something. There must be a cause worth $1,000. He won't care as long as the request is coming from a woman. You'd be amazed."

Back on the upper level, Ralph continued to give Stewart a few more pointers.

"Another thing chicks like is when you act and talk rough. For example, just rustle her hair so that it looks disheveled. Then smiling add, 'just what I like, you wild thing, you.'"

Stewart was astonished at such brash words. "That

would be so unlike me to say that."

"That's the idea. Don't be yourself. It's called 'macho,' like an image thing. Got my drift there, fella?" Ralph advised.

"Not really," a confused Stewart replied.

"Trust me. Once you get in the habit of being someone that you are not, you'll fit right in with the ladies. Women don't want reality. They want Hollywood, action and adventure. The last thing you want to do is come across as a caring, empathizing, conversation-filled human being."

"Wow. No wonder things went so bad last night. I was trying to be so polite and gentlemanly."

"All wrong. We're coming to our first stop. Go get her, Tarzan."

"I'm game." Stewart poked out his chest and sat tall.

"Correction. She's game," Ralph grinned.

14

Sonny announced, "This is Bull Street, where you can browse and shop a little at the unique gift shops and sip some refreshing beverages. Please return to the bus in about two hours."

The bus stopped and the passengers exited the bus.

"Look, Debbie, there's a nice boutique store. Let's go in there." Gloria walked Debbie briskly to the shop.

Stewart and Ralph exited the bus. "I don't see Debbie. Anyway, it's a good place to give Bread some exercise." Stewart searched for a place to walk Bread.

"I do see an outdoor café shop. Let's grab a pop or snack while we look for her," Ralph suggested.

"What for? We can get all the food and beverages we want back at the hotel. Besides, I brought some of it in my lunch bag," Stewart countered. "Have some?" Stewart offered some of his room service food to Ralph.

"Save it. Go on without me. I'll be sitting right here, looking at the chicks walk by."

"I'll be back in thirty minutes?" Stewart checked his watch.

"No problem," Ralph's waved his hand at Stewart in one direction with his eyes focused on the cute waitress approaching him from the other direction.

"Come on Bread." Stewart walked Bread down the sidewalk.

Bread tagged along with Stewart.

"Look, there's a bookstore. Maybe they will have Savannah area cookbooks," he said to Bread.

Gloria and Debbie shopped at the boutique.

"This would be great on you. Try it on," Gloria said to Debbie.

"I don't know. Don't you think the white polka-dot on vivid orange spandex halter top and neon lime green hip-hugging stretch Capri pants kind of clash?" Debbie asked.

"Not if you tie them all together with this silk gold scarf," Gloria replied as she handed Debbie some matching three-inch loop gold earrings. "Just try them on. It'll work."

"Oh well. Why not?" Debbie said as she took the pieces into the dressing room.

"What do you think?" Debbie asked, as she emerged from the dressing room.

"Perfect! Stewart will find you irresistible in that ensemble."

"He'll just have to wait in line though with the other fellas."

"Honey, you will definitely get noticed."

"I'll get noticed all right. But will it be good or bad? There's not a curve hidden." Debbie stared into the mirror.

"That looks stunning." The saleswoman continued, "The colors say 'wow!'"

"She'll get it. Do you have some scissors to cut the tags off? She wants to wear it out of the store."

"Great. I'll be right back with that and the sales

receipt."

"Are you sure Stewart will like this?" Debbie asked again.

"There's only one way to find out."

"Here you go. Sign here and I'll put your old clothes in the shopping bag," the saleswoman said.

Debbie signed and left the store in her new look.

"Strut a little like this." Gloria demonstrated an exaggerated hip switch.

Debbie practiced switching her hips from side to side without falling off of her four-inch high wedge sandals. The gold dangling tassels on the top of her sandals tickled her feet as they swayed with her every move.

"Like this?" Debbie wobbled a few steps.

"You've got it."

The sun was hot and it was high noon.

"At least this head scarf provides some relief from the sun," Debbie concluded.

"I'm thirsty. Let's get a lemonade or something," Gloria suggested.

"Good idea," Debbie said, wobbling down the street in her new high heel sandals and body-hugging Capri pants. Some of the men whistled as they walked passed them.

"I thought whistling went out of style years ago. It's been a long time since that happened to me. As a matter of fact, it's never happened to me before," Debbie said.

"I told you. Men will just love you for how you look. When it comes to male-female relationships, brains do not count," Gloria educated Debbie.

"There's an outside café over there. Let's try that. My feet need a rest from these high heels," Debbie noted.

Gloria looked over to the café and saw Ralph on the far end flirting with the waitress. "That's a good place." She pointed over to the café. They sat at a table on the other side of the café, facing Ralph.

"What kind of beverage would you like?" the waitress asked Gloria and Debbie.

"I'd like some lemonade please," Gloria ordered.

"Me too. Thanks."

"They will be right up," the waitress obliged.

"Look at the time, Bread. We've been standing here reading these cookbooks for more than thirty minutes. I think I can remember some of the recipes so it won't be necessary to buy the book. Let's go. I want to talk to Debbie before we get on the bus."

Less than a block away, Stewart spotted Ralph at the café where he left him.

Just about this time, Ralph was looking around to see what other ladies he could check out. He quickly noticed Gloria. He mumbled to himself, "who is she sitting with?"

Gloria saw Stewart walking down the street to the café.

Gloria motioned with her eyes to Ralph and mouthed the word 'Debbie,' so that he knew whom she was sitting with.

"Excuse me, Debbie. I've got to go to the ladies room."

While inside the café, she peered through the

window to see what was going to happen next.

"Hi, Ralph. Sorry it took me longer than thirty minutes to get back here. Any sign of Debbie?"

"Yes. She is sitting over there," Ralph pointed.

"Where? I don't see her," Stewart looked for Debbie.

"Over there in the gold scarf tied around her head," Ralph nodded in Debbie's direction.

"That's Debbie? Are you sure?"

"Better hurry before some other guy beats you to the punch." Ralph grabbed Stewart by the t-shirt and pushed him in Debbie's direction. "Remember what I told you," Ralph reminded Stewart.

"Okay. Here it goes." Stewart took a deep breath as he walked slowly to Debbie. Stewart leaned over and placed his hand on Debbie's bare right shoulder.

Instinctively, Debbie grabbed his hand, twisted it over her head while she abruptly stood up, turned around, knocked the chair away with a loud sound. She rolled Stewart's stomach over her back, lifting him completely off the ground. Next, she rolled him back to the ground allowing him to fall flat on his face back to the ground.

Gloria saw the whole thing from the window as she giggled uncontrollably.

The wait staff rushed to Debbie's rescue.

"Are you all right ma'am? Is this gentleman bothering you?"

Ralph placed his hands over his mouth as he tried to contain his laughter.

In total shock, Debbie looked down at Stewart who staggered as he rose up from a now sitting position.

"Is that you, Stewart? I'm so sorry. I didn't know." Debbie attempted to help Stewart get up off the ground.

"I can get up by myself. What did you do that for?" the disheveled Stewart snapped.

The waiters went back to their duties.

"I am truly sorry. I didn't know it was you. I just have this self-defense karate skill."

"I thought you were for non-violence," Stewart grumbled, as he gingerly moved to sit in a chair.

"I am. You had no business sneaking up on me like that."

"I wasn't sneaking up on you. I was coming to talk to you."

The waitress returned and asked Stewart, "What kind of beverage would you like sir?"

"I'll just have water, with a twist of lime, thanks."

"Okay."

"Well, you have a strange way of doing that," Debbie said with annoyance.

"I'm strange? What is that you are wearing? It's not what you had on when you got on the bus."

"Are you calling me strange? Why did you come over here?

Maybe I should finish what I started when I floored you," she retorted.

"Finish what? We haven't started anything, chick," he shot back.

"Chick? Chick?" I'm not a chick. I'm a woman, in case you haven't noticed," she argued.

"Oh, I've noticed all right. You could be noticed a

mile away in that get up."

"Do you have any more insults before I tell you to leave?"

"Yes. As a matter of fact, I do!" he said.

"What's that?"

"Let's change the subject," the disheveled Stewart said.

"Okay. I need $1,000."

"Money? For what!"

"Well, huh, or... to save the pheasants in Detroit."

"Pheasants? What pheasants?"

"They are being displaced by urban renewal. We have to find another home for them to live."

"I never thought you'd be a gold digger, like the rest of them. No way." Stewart tightly folded his arms and turned his head away from Debbie.

"Gold digger? Rest of them? Just leave right now. You, you...man!" Debbie furiously shouted.

Gloria, still at a distance, winked in victory to Ralph. Ralph sat back in his patio chair sipping lemonade and watched the whole thing with a cool smile.

Suddenly, Butter ran off down the street meowing.

"Bark, bark, bark." Bread ran down the street after Butter.

"Where are you going Butter? Come back here." Debbie stopped arguing with Stewart and ran after Butter.

"Stop chasing Butter, Bread. You come back here right now." Stewart dropped his arguing with Debbie as he also ran in hot pursuit of Bread.

Butter and Bread slowed down. Just as Stewart and Debbie got within a few yards, they sped off in another direction together, barking and meowing. They got just so far so as not to lose sight of Stewart and Debbie. As soon as Stewart and Debbie got closer to them, they ran off again.

Debbie's gold headscarf started falling off her head around her neck. Her shoulder strap broke. Debbie ran so fast she didn't have time to fix it. Her right ankle turned as she ran in the grass through a nearby park, and the wedge sandal came off.

She leaned down to get it, but Stewart grabbed her arm and said, "Leave it. We don't have time. We've got to catch them before they get lost."

Debbie was limping now with one shoe on and one left behind in the soft grass. They chased Bread and Butter through a water sprinkler system and kept running.

Back at the café, "Did you see that?" Gloria asked Ralph.

"They were so mad at each other. I hope we didn't overdo it," she added.

"You're a genius, doll. It was beautiful. When they get back, I'll be there for my Debbie."

"I'll be there for my Stewart," Gloria said pulling out her compact mirror and freshening up her lipstick.

"There they are!" Stewart shouted, pointing near the large water fountain in the park.

"Hurry, we've got to get them before they get in the fountain!"

Debbie yelled, as she tossed the other shoe off to run faster. She was almost out of breath. Her clothes were disheveled and her hair was all over her head.

Stewart ran to the fountain and just as he got to the edge, Bread and Butter moved toward the middle of the fountain."

"Look. They stopped in the middle of the water over there," Stewart told Debbie.

"Go get them," Debbie directed Stewart.

"Me? Oh no. We'll go get them together," Stewart reached for Debbie's hand as he waded further into the fountain's waters.

By now, Bread and Butter and Stewart and Debbie were drenched.

"Gotcha," he said to Bread, grabbing his leash.

"Gotcha too," she said to Butter.

The four of them were standing in a shower of the water fountain when they noticed that people were clapping and laughing at them. Debbie was soaking wet with her clothes half off and bare feet. Stewart was soaking wet with a torn t-shirt and dirty pants.

They stood still for a moment. They started laughing and Stewart decided to pick Debbie up and carry her out of the fountain like prince charming rescuing his beautiful princess, along with a few pets in tow behind. All four sat down for a rest on the lawn to dry out a little and laugh about the entire episode.

"Can you believe Butter went into the water as much as she hates water?" She laughed in disbelief.

"Can you believe Bread jumped in too?" Stewart laughed back.

"I can't remember when I ran so fast and so much," she chuckled.

"Same here. Nor when I've had so much fun." he smiled with eyes intense on her.

"Me too," she smiled back with eyes focused on him.

"If it weren't for Bread and Butter running off, we'd still be arguing at the café." He laid back on the green lawn in total relaxation.

"Look at us now." She relaxed and laid beside him. There was a moment of silence, as they both took a deep breath and sigh of relief.

"That's exactly what I'm doing. Debbie, you look beautiful no matter what you wear. You'll always be beautiful to me," Stewart said softly.

"Stewart, I've been attracted to you from the moment I saw you on the plane." She gazed into his eyes.

"Maybe I can solve the pheasant problem. I make a mean pheasant soup," he offered.

"Let me think about that," she laughed.

"Look at the time. We'd better get back to the bus stop."

Stewart helped Debbie up.

"Thanks."

They walked back to the bus stop, laughing and talking, with Bread and Butter trailing behind them on their leashes.

Soon they were back at the cafe and bus stop.

Gloria and Ralph rubbed their eyes as they took a double look at the happy couple.

"What happened?" Gloria asked Ralph.

"You had a really dumb idea. I could have told you it wouldn't work," Ralph complained.

"Dumb idea. Dumb idea," piped the parakeet, Talker.

Bread and Butter sat peacefully with Debbie and Stewart by their sides on a bench by the bus stop. Debbie found her old shoes in the shopping bag and put them back on. She found her comfortable soft flowing blouse and slipped that over her now completely strapless halter.

All parties returned to the tour bus, which had just pulled up and opened its doors.

"We hope you enjoyed your stop," Sonny gleefully piped.

"Did you know that Savannah was voted the top romantic city in the South?"

"Now he tells me," Gloria mumbled. She returned to her seat next to Debbie without saying a word.

"Gloria, I guess your idea about how to dress certainly got his attention and worked. Thanks for the help. Stewart and I are talking again."

"Don't mention it," Gloria tersely said.

Ralph sat by Stewart.

"Man, I took charge, and Debbie loved it. Things where rocky in the beginning. Thanks. You really know what you're talking about," Stewart gratefully said to Ralph.

"Just don't overdo it," a less than enthusiastic Ralph concurred.

Gloria, disgusted at the failed scheme, got up and walked to the back of the bus. Abby noticed that Gloria was a little down.

"Did you enjoy the sightseeing?" Abby probed.

"It was a disaster, thank you," Gloria lamented.

"What do you mean?" Abby motioned Gloria to sit down next to her rather than return immediately to her seat.

"I like this guy, however, he likes someone else. That's all," Gloria explained.

"Give it time. Things will work out the way it is meant to be. Just trust God to give you patience."

"Time and patience are things I don't have much of right now."

"You will be surprised how quickly God can operate. You just have to work with His time schedule, okay, dear?"

"I'll try," Gloria halfheartedly replied before returning to her seat.

"Thank you for taking our Savannah tour." Sonny stopped the bus in front of the hotel.

"After you get freshened up," Abby announced, "the Pets-by-the-Sea Hotel has a special surprise tonight for all of our hotel guests."

As Stewart exited the bus he asked Abby, "Is there going to be a charge for this 'surprise'?"

"Absolutely not. Not a penny extra," Abby smiled.

"I'll be there. Where did you say it was?"

"I didn't. Just be in the lobby at 5:00 p.m." Abby said, not wanting to give the surprise away.

"Okay," Stewart walked over to Debbie.

"Want to go to the special surprise tonight?"

"I'd love to."

"Great. I'll see you in the lobby at 5:00 p.m."

Stewart walked back to his room with Bread for a mid-day rest and more free room service. Gloria and Ralph returned to their rooms too.

15

It was Tuesday at 5:00 p.m., time for the surprise evening out. All the hotel guests boarded the hotel buses with their pets. After a short ten-minute ride, the bus stopped in front of a homeless shelter.

"This is it, folks. Watch your step as you leave the bus," warned the bus driver.

"What is this?" Ralph complained.

"It's a homeless shelter and soup kitchen and we are going to prepare and serve the evening dinner for the homeless," David said.

"I don't do kitchens. I don't do cook. I only eat," Ralph fussed. "Take me back to the hotel," he ordered the bus driver.

"I'm sorry sir, but I've been instructed not to leave until all the passengers return."

"Hello, Ralph," Abby noticed that he was the last one off the bus.

"Hi, Abby," Ralph stubbornly said.

"We'd love for you to join us. There are some people here who really look forward to your visit," Abby gently coaxed Ralph.

"I don't mean to be disrespectful, but I'm not cooking."

"That's okay. Just share a little of your time, please?" Abby politely asked.

"Okay. I don't want to be here all night. I've got other things to do."

"Yes, I know. Right this way, through those doors." Abby pointed to the entrance of the building.

Stewart was already inside.

"I paid for a vacation, not this shelter work," Stewart mumbled to Debbie.

Debbie reminded him that Second Corinthians 9:6 said: "'*He which soweth bountifully shall reap bountifully.*' Your giving will not go to waste."

"Who said that?" Stewart quipped.

"Paul."

"Do I know him?" Stewart joked.

"There you are." The Homeless Shelter Director Stephen shook Stewart's hand.

"We've been waiting for you. Come this way, over here."

"Sir, this shelter thing is nice for the homeless, but I paid $10,000 for a vacation with my pet. I am to be served, not serve," Stewart reminded Stephen.

"I see." Stephen scratched his head.

Just then, David walked over to Stephen.

Stephen whispered in his ear, "I thought you told him that he was going to cook. We've given our regular cook the night off. What are we going to do now?"

David whispered back into Stephen's ear, "Don't worry. Have faith. I'll handle this."

"Okay."

Silently, David called on the Lord for guidance. "Dear Lord, I need a cook. Can you help me out here?"

"How can we get back to the hotel?" Stewart asked.

"Have you seen the kitchen?" David asked.

"No. Let me explain something, David. I go to church every Sunday. I even tithe, no small amount, I might add. Why should I do this too?" Stewart questioned David as he followed him into the kitchen.

"I hear you're a good cook." David continued into the kitchen.

"Yes. I'm one of the best, as a matter of fact," Stewart said.

"Follow me in here. I'd like to show you something." David guided him as they entered into the homeless shelter's large kitchen with commercial sized range and oven. Nearby was the large side-by-side stainless steel refrigerator.

"Here. Try this on," David said. He placed a head chef one foot high tall white hat on Stewart's head. Dave motioned Stephen to proceed with a tour of the kitchen, which was well stocked with appliance and kitchen supplies.

"Look at this! Have you ever seen such a beauty?" Stephen beamed.

"This is the most impressive commercial kitchen I've ever seen. It reminds me of my kitchen." Stewart's eyes lit up.

"It's all yours." Stephen waved his hand across the span of the kitchen area.

"What?" Stewart said in awe.

"You are the head chef for the evening. Just tell us what to do so that we can feed everyone tonight. We have all kinds of food. Just pick out what you like, and tell us how to fix it."

Stewart opened the refrigerator and saw a wide selection of foods. Then he went to the pantry shelves and saw a myriad of spices and accoutrements. He walked over to the large commercial range and saw the same luxury brand stove that he had in his kitchen at home.

By this time, Debbie entered the kitchen and commented, "I hope someone can cook, because we have a lot of hungry people out there."

Stewart looked at Debbie and asked, "Do you like gourmet food?"

"Yes. Where do we start?" Debbie volunteered.

"Where are the aprons? We'll start with appetizers." Stewart was beginning to warm to his role as head chef for the evening.

"Praise the Lord!" Stephen grabbed a clean apron from the kitchen clothes hook and tied it around Stewart.

Ralph was sitting in a corner of the dining room, sulking and tapping his drumsticks on the plain white plastic table in boredom. A little boy approached.

"Can I play with your chopsticks?"

Ralph eyed the child up and down and noticed that he had old torn clothes, run down old tennis shoes with holes in the upper toe area.

"Aren't you hungry? Go eat," Ralph sternly said.

"I'm not hungry. Can I play with your chopsticks?" the child persisted.

"These are not chopsticks. They are drumsticks," Ralph corrected the little boy.

"They don't look like chicken to me," the boy

curiously noted. "Young fella, this is not from a chicken, it's from a tree," Ralph explained.

"Then why don't they call it a tree stick?" the boy asked.

"Because it plays on drums."

"I don't see any drums. Where are your drums?"

"In Detroit,"

"Then why do you have drumsticks and no drums?" the little boy asked.

"Here, let me see you play a tune or two." Ralph gingerly allowed the boy to hold the drumsticks.

The boy started to tap very faintly on the table as his eyes lit up. "How am I doing?"

"Great for a beginner. Let me show you how to hold the sticks so you can do even better." The little boy watched intensely how Ralph held the sticks. He mimicked Ralph's grip of the sticks. "Not bad. I'll be right back. Don't go anywhere with my drumsticks." Ralph quickly walked over into the kitchen.

"You've decided to help us back here," Stephen said.

"Got any empty pots and pans?" Ralph asked, ignoring his comment.

"Sure we do. Look under there by the sink."

"Great. These will do just fine," Ralph said, as he walked out of the kitchen with four various sizes of pots, pans and tops. He returned to the little boy who was still holding his drumsticks. He reached for the sticks as the boy started to frown. "Watch this," Ralph said as he turned each pan upside down and proceeded to play various drumbeats on the pans with the sticks.

"Can I try it?"

"Sure. Go ahead and play something."

By this time, Gloria turned on the radio and the guests started clapping their hands to the beat and the music. Gloria started singing. People were having a great time. She went over to a table to sit down for a few minutes after singing a song. She sat by an old lady who was admiring Gloria's jewelry, especially one of her many gold bangles.

"You like this kind of jewelry?" Gloria observantly asked the old lady.

"It's very nice," the old lady meekly said.

Gloria took off a few of her bracelets to give to her.

The old lady started to cry. "Thank you, my child. I haven't owned a piece of jewelry in twenty years. God bless you for your kindness." The old lady bowed her head down.

"You're welcome. Now, now, dry those tears," Gloria tried to comfort her.

"It's not easy these days. My first husband died. My second husband left me for another woman. I have no children."

"Go shop!" Gloria proclaimed.

"I have no money," the old lady said with a puzzled look on her face.

"I don't mean that kind of shopping." Gloria turned her head and eyes over to an old man sitting alone in a corner of the room.

"I think he's got your number, the way I saw him looking at you."

"Where? I don't have a telephone?"

"Why don't you ask him how did he get your

number? Go ahead." Gloria shushed the old lady in the direction of the old man, who looked as lonely as the old lady.

The old lady got up and walked over to the man.

He smiled at her. She smiled back.

"You go girl," Gloria laughed.

In an amazing time of just sixty minutes, Stewart had orchestrated the most delicious meal any restaurant could serve, all for the benefit of the homeless.

He turned to Debbie, "It's done. They are going to love it, I hope."

"I'm sure they will. It looks and smells great."

"Somehow, this accomplishment feels far greater than any big real estate closing deal I've ever made. How do you explain that?"

"Maybe it's because money can't buy this feeling of serving others in need, rather than ourselves," Debbie suggested.

"The food is ready to be served," Stephen announced. "Mr. Shepherd, will you do the honor of blessing this food?"

"May we all bow our heads for prayer? Dear Heavenly Father, thank you for this special opportunity to serve you through serving others. Like Jesus said, those who feed the hungry, feed Jesus. As we bless others, You bless us. Thank you Father for your obedient sheep, the nourishing food and your love. Amen."

"This is really delicious. What is it?" asked one homeless person.

"It's lobster with clam relish," Stewart beamed over one of his appetizers.

Stephen strapped a breadbasket on top of Bread's back like a saddle. Bread went around from table to table, allowing the homeless to retrieve their bread. Some of them took a small piece and gave it to Bread to eat. He eagerly chomped it down.

Butter dashed in and out from under the tables, while being chased by the children. When they caught her they patted and rubbed her on the back until she purred sweet enjoyment. Then she dashed off, until they caught her again.

"Talker wants a cracker!" said Talker. So the homeless shared some of their bread with him.

Gloria's Goldies swam around in their fishbowl, oblivious to the strife and turmoil written so clearly in the faces of the homeless. One person, so stressed and tense, could barely eat her food. Nibbling at a piece here and there, she happened to gaze into the fishbowl. As she sat there observing their smooth movements, her shoulders relaxed and calm crept over her face.

"Can I feed the fish?" the lady asked Gloria.

"Sure." Gloria handed the lady a small carton of fish food to shake into the bowl.

The evening was almost over. The shelter people gathered up their things to return to their sleeping cots. The hotel guests wiped the last table and swept the last corner of the floor.

Stewart completed his assignment in the kitchen, leaving it spotless. Debbie, who had assisted with making the meal, hung up her apron.

Just before the bus returned to take the hotel guests back, a little boy, about seven years old, came up to Stewart and Bread with a small ball in his hand.

"Here. I want Bread to have it so that he will have

something to play with and remember me by," the boy humbly said, giving his only toy to Stewart for Bread.

The other guests' eyes swelled with tears as they watched.

There was silence in the room. Stewart looked at the ball.

As he hesitated, Debbie gently placed her hand on Stewart's shoulder and whispered in his ear, "It would mean so much to him."

Stewart reached out and received the ball from the little boy's hands.

"Bread and I thank you. We'll take good care of the ball. Bread likes balls and will truly enjoy playing with this one. You are a very special little boy. What's your name?" he asked.

The little boy smiled upon handing over his ball and replied, "My name is James, like in the book of James in the Bible." The little boy skipped off and away with the biggest smile a little boy could ever have. The hotel guests looked on.

There wasn't a dry eye among them.

"This is it, folks. We're back at the hotel. Thanks for your spirit of cooperation and the very fruitful use of your talents," David said. All the passengers on the bus clapped their hands in appreciation to David and Abby and, most importantly, for the experience at the Homeless Shelter.

"Thank you for the surprise," Debbie said while exiting the bus.

"The pleasure was all ours," Abby smiled.

"You truly made this vacation special. By the way, who paid for all that food?" Stewart asked.

"You did. We take a portion of the money from every vacation package to contribute food to the shelter," David explained.

"That's nice. Next time, buy some drums while you're at it," Ralph joked.

"And they could use a few permanent pets to keep, like goldfish," Gloria suggested.

"Great ideas. Thank you. Have a good night," David replied.

"We already did," Stewart said.

"Do you think they got the message that there are more important things in life than being served?" David asked Abby before retiring for the evening.

"I think so. I know I saw a lot of love, kindness and caring by everyone. Service brings a kind of spiritual fulfillment."

"You're right. By the way, honey, got any snacks tonight?"

"Yes. Always, dear."

16

"Welcome to the Wednesday Breakfast Bible Class. Our teacher for today is our very own David Shepherd. He's not only the manager of our wonderful Pets-by-the-Sea Hotel, but the founder and owner, so he gets to do whatever he wants, unlike the people who work for him," Timothy, turned announcer, joked.

David gave him a stern look and motioned him to continue, though cautiously.

"David is an ordained minister, and has been for quite some time. Looking at his pot belly, I'd say he is pretty ancient too," Timothy laughed with his hyena laugh. David stood up to proceed before Timothy finished.

"One final note. He is married with one child, me. So you know he's a good person, just by looking at the fruits of his labor, or should I say, Mom's labor." Timothy almost rolled over in laughter.

"Thank you, son. That will be enough." David wore his white clergy collar and black conservative, short sleeve leisure suit for the Bible class. He took a sip of ice water.

"Good morning class. Thank you for taking the time out during your vacation with us to spend a little time with God's Word. Before we begin our Bible lesson for today, please indulge me to tell you a little bit about our programs here at Pets-by-the-Sea Hotel."

"This hotel is my ministry. However, I couldn't do

anything without your presence and participation in the many activities we plan for you and your loving pets throughout the week. I want you to know that our services here are five-star quality.

Even with that expense, we still manage to donate a considerable amount of money to those less fortunate, like the homeless shelters and animal shelters. Additional donations for these causes are always welcomed."

Stewart whispered in Debbie's ear, "He's got to be kidding about 'additional donations' after what we paid to get here."

"Pay? Did you pay to come here?" Debbie whispered back to Stewart in fun.

"What do you mean by that?"

"Just joking."

In the audience was a sinister-looking woman with sunglasses and an oversized hat, the brim partially hiding her face. She adjusted her voice-activated miniature microphone under her blazer in silence.

David continued, "Let us pray. Dear Heavenly Father, bless this class. May they seek, find, receive and accept your Holy Word. Amen."

"The title of today's lesson is, 'Why Forgive?'"

"What a bummer. I thought we were going to talk about sex," Ralph mumbled.

"Sex. Talk Sex," Talker blurted out.

"Shush," Ralph told Talker.

David commented, "We're used to pets making noises around here."

He continued, "The key verses can be found in the

book of Matthew, Chapter 6, verses 14 and 15. It reads: *'For if ye forgive men their trespasses, your heavenly Father will also forgive you: But if ye forgive not men their trespasses, neither will your Father forgive your trespasses.'* I'm sure everyone in the audience today has at some time or other been forgiven and has forgiven others. I don't think that there is any doubt among you that there are times when forgiveness is appropriate and given freely without hesitation or thought. The mere fact that everyone at this hotel owns a pet, tells me that you know something about forgiveness. Certainly, when you are training your pets or even protecting them from harm, they mess up.

Nevertheless, you forgive them so fast that you often forget that you forgave."

Butter crept under Debbie's chair to an inconspicuous spot. Bread comforted Butter.

David continued, "So the questions in my mind, and perhaps yours also, are not do you forgive, but who do you forgive, when do you forgive, and why do you forgive? Let's begin with the first question, 'Who do you forgive?'"

Timothy blurted out, "Everyone."

"The next question is, 'When do you forgive?'"

Timothy yelled out, "Every time."

"The final and most important question that I want someone other than my son to respond to is, 'Why do you forgive?' If you don't fully understand why you should forgive, you won't be motivated to comply with the first two mandates.

Is there anyone in the audience, who is not part of the staff or my relative, who cares to take a stab at the answer? But before you do, I want to tell you a story.

"There was a business owner, who owed a bank $52,800,000 in secured loans, having mortgaged his home and business.

The bank had just completed doing an audit of its accounts receivables and noticed that this business owner's account was seriously delinquent in paying on the loan by several months. The banker called in the business owner to immediately pay all of the $52,800,000 or else the banker would take him to court to repossess everything that he owned. The banker also threatened to file criminal charges for fraud. The business owner could go to jail, if found guilty of the charges."

David continued, "At the thought of going to jail, the business owner pleaded with the banker to not file a complaint, because he would make every effort to repay him every penny.

The banker felt compassion for the business owner and, realizing that the business owner would never get out of debt with the terms he proposed, forgave the entire debt and decided not to file charges. This allowed the business owner to make a fresh start of his life."

David continued, "The next day the business owner was going through his accounts receivables and noticed that a customer owed him $440. The business owner went to the customer's home and angrily demanded that he pay the entire $440 on the spot or else he would sue him that very day. When the customer begged the business owner for just a little more time to pay the entire amount, the business owner started choking the customer. The customer's friends had to grab the business owner off the customer. The business owner went in a huff straight to court to file a complaint against the customer for non-payment of a debt."

Stewart whispered in Debbie's ear, "I could do a lot with $440."

Debbie whispered back, "I'm sure you could. However, that's not the point of the story."

David continued, "Word got back to the banker about what the business owner had done to the customer. This made the banker very angry. He immediately filed charges against the banker for the $52,800,000 debt. This resulted in the business owner going to jail, where he would stay until all his debt was repaid."

Ralph asked, "So what's your point?"

David explained, "If we don't forgive our brothers and sisters, our heavenly Father won't forgive us. The consequences would be much worse than what the business owner suffered.

"There are additional reasons as to why we should forgive. Let's hear some of them from you. Why should we forgive?"

Stewart raised his hand. "I think the reason why we should forgive others is because sometimes it makes good business sense. You never know what other customers are watching how you treat a customer who has fallen on hard times."

"Good answer. Any other answers?"

Debbie raised her hand.

"It makes you feel better so that you are not the 'bad guy.'

You kind of get it off your chest, so to speak. You release it and let it go. It's healthier for you physically and mentally."

"Another good answer. Is there anyone else who wants to answer this question of 'why?'"

Ralph raised his hand, from the back of the room, and responded, "Because if you care about someone and want to get along with them, it breaks the ice. It allows you to heat up the relationship, if you know what I mean,"

"That's an interesting way to put it. However, I hope we don't forgive just for, how can I put this delicately?"

"Sex?" Ralph blurted out.

"Let's call it 'favors.' Any other reasons to forgive?"

Gloria raised her hand and added, "Because even though God loves us, He will separate the forgivers from the unforgivers. For example, my two goldfish get along just fine, so I keep them together."

"Yes. That is a very important motivation for us to forgive: in order to avoid alienation from others and God," David concluded.

"We've heard several answers. Which answer is correct?" said David.

Before anyone else could respond, Timothy said tersely, "All of them."

"That's correct, son. All of them. Just remember when you know the 'why' you will find the 'way.'" The pets started fidgeting.

"Let us pray. Dear Heavenly Father, You are a loving Father and are all knowing and all seeing. So watch over the flock; keep them safe in this journey called life and forgive them for their sins, as they have forgiven others. Amen."

"Class dismissed!" Timothy gleefully shouted.

Everyone started running to the exit like a herd of buffalos, except Debbie and Ralph.

Stewart, who was also dashing out, told Debbie, "I'll see you in the lobby at 2:00 p.m. for the trip to the beach party. Got to get Bread some lunch first."

"Okay."

Gloria rushed off to the Pet Gift Shop. "I wonder if they have any accessories for my Goldies?" she said to her fish, who looked at her from their fishbowl for a moment before resuming their rounds.

Debbie lingered behind after class. "Thank you, David. I really needed that message today."

"You're welcome, my child. Now go and have fun and forgive."

"I will do just that."

Ralph waited in the back of the room as Debbie approached the exit door near him. When she was about ten feet away, Ralph asked, "Now that you are in this forgiving mood, can I take you to lunch?"

"No. I forgive you and now I forget you," Debbie blurted out before she realized it.

Ralph cleared his voice. "That was cold, Debbie. I liked it better when you just floored me." He held his head down.

"I don't mean to hurt you. I'm just not interested in you."

"I get it. I'm boring huh? Maybe if I take you on an exciting date, you will want to be with me."

"Maybe. But right now, I'm seeing someone else."

"Did I hear a maybe? I'll go see if I can find something exciting to do and get back to you." He waited for an answer.

"I've got to go."

"Save some lovin' for me," Ralph said to Debbie's turned back.

Debbie walked away without further comment.

17

Ralph approached Martha at the hotel's front desk.

"Do you know where a guy can take his woman on an exciting date around here?"

"No," Martha replied.

"Do you know who might know?"

"No."

Just then Timothy walked through the lobby.

"Hey, Timothy. Come over here." Ralph waved his arm motioning to Timothy to approach him.

"Yes, sir?"

"I'm looking for an exciting date. What's jumping around Savannah? I want a hot spot, if you know what I mean."

"Let me think. I know where the fish are jumping and the perfect hot spot, where you can have excitement and cool down at the same time."

"Great! What?"

"Tybee Island. They have the Tybee Island Marine Science Center, where the fish are lively and they have the hot beach where you can cool off in the ocean for a swim."

"Very funny," Ralph snapped.

"No. I'm serious. Don't tell my Dad, but I've had a lot of exciting dates there," Timothy spoke softly out of

Martha's earshot.

"Kid, you stay out of trouble and away from that beach. How do I get there?"

Timothy laughed his hyena laugh.

"That's our afternoon planned activity. The hotel van leaves every hour for the beach starting at 2:00 p.m."

"I'll be there."

Ralph called Debbie.

"Hello," Debbie replied.

"Hi. I found an exciting place that we can go. What time can I pick you up?" Ralph asked optimistically.

"Ralph? Why don't you check it out without me, just to see if it is the right place? Okay?" Debbie stalled any future encounter with Ralph.

"Sure. I'll do that. Then we could..."

"Excuse me, I've got to go. Bye." Debbie hung up the phone.

"I'll check out the place and get back to you," Ralph said to the empty line. Ralph hung up the phone and thought out loud, "I can't go by myself. What would a guy like me look like at a beach with no chick?"

Ralph called Gloria.

"Hello?" Gloria answered.

"I know of a great beach party. Do you want to go?" Ralph asked.

"She stood you up, huh?"

"I'm asking you. Do you want to go or not?" Ralph said with irritation.

"Why not? I'm not in the mood to go to the beach

party alone either, just to watch the love couple."

"Be ready in thirty minutes."

"I'll be ready. Just show up on time."

"Dress sexy," Ralph teased.

"Don't get any ideas. I'm just agreeing to go to the beach party with you. That's all. Agreed?"

"Only if you keep your hands to yourself. I know I'm irresistible," Ralph quipped.

"It's a deal. See you," Gloria laughed.

"Isn't this the most beautiful beachfront?" Stewart commented to Debbie as they arrived in the hotel van on Tybee Island's very large public beach. The warm moist breeze and smell of sea salt was like a refreshing sauna.

Debbie wore stylish white, loose-fitting long pants, with a light jersey scoop neck, elbow length white top. She had her oversized straw hat and basic white leather sandals. Her simple, sleek lines could be on a fashion magazine cover. Stewart was wearing the same thing he had on at the Bible class: navy cotton trousers and a plain white short sleeved shirt.

"Got your camera?" he asked her. "I'd like to take a picture of you and Butter."

"Here it is, in my tote bag. Mind if I snap a picture of you and Bread?"

"Not at all."

Debbie then posed with Butter in her arms.

While posing and taking pictures of each other, another visitor walked by and snapped pictures of the various pets and their owners at the beach party. Debbie noticed that it was the same person that took pictures at the dining room.

Abby greeted the guests. "Welcome to our beach party. If I can be of any assistance, just ask. I'll be mingling with the other guests."

The beach party included playground slides and water slides by the pool. There were basketball and volleyball games for the pets and their owners. Debbie and Stewart chatted as they walked along the pier during the beach party. Bread and Butter trailed behind them on their leashes.

"This is so peaceful. It's hard to imagine that there is a care in the world," Debbie mused. They both gazed into the pristine waters lapping on the boardwalk's pier.

"This is relaxing. I feel like I'm a thousand miles away from the hustle and bustle of work," Stewart said walking side by side with Debbie.

"We are a thousand miles from work. Have you ever wanted to just chuck it all and live like a beach bum?"

"No. I don't mind working. I've been doing it all my adult life, so when I retire, I won't be a beach bum."

"I guess hard work is fine, when you have a goal to it. One thing I like about you is that you are so logical and know how to plan things for the future." She looked into Stewart's eyes.

"Thanks for the compliment. When I do take a break, this is the kind of break I want to take, that is walking down a beach with a pretty woman like you. I feel so relaxed talking to you, Debbie. Everyday is like a vacation when I'm around you."

"I feel the same about you."

Stewart turned to his dog and pulled out a biscuit, "Want a piece of biscuit, Bread?"

Bread jumped up high to catch the tossed biscuit and

quickly gobbled it down.

Butter tugged on her leash slightly pulling further inland from the water and where some of the pets were playing.

Feeling Butter's tug and sensing that she wanted to get off the pier, Debbie asked Stewart, "What's that crowd doing over there? It looks like they are playing games with their pets."

"Let's go and see."

18

Back at the hotel, Ralph and Gloria, with Talker and the Goldies, took the 3:00 p.m. hotel van to Tybee Island.

"So what are we going to do about Stewart and Debbie?" Gloria asked Ralph.

Gloria readjusted her tight orange and yellow wraparound, multi-length gauze fabric tie-skirt over her hot pink skimpy bikini.

"Why couldn't you wear something a little more revealing, sugar?" Ralph joked.

"Because if I did, you couldn't handle yourself. Let's stick to the subject here, remember? Why we came to Savannah? To catch our mates?"

"Everything you've tried so far has failed," he informed her.

"I'm going to keep trying. Are you in or out?"

"I'm out, but I'd like to be in," he grinned.

"Okay. This is what we will do when we get to the beach party. We'll pretend we are not together so that Stewart and Debbie won't see us talking to each other."

"Let me get this straight, honey dumpling. We'll be together, but they won't see us together?" Ralph asked.

"You've got it."

"No. You've lost it." Ralph shook his head.

Gloria explained further, "We still have to communicate."

"How are we going to do that, if we are not together?"

"It'll be like you see in the movies. We'll pretend like we don't know each other, but talk behind the bushes or with our backs to each other."

"I don't know you, apple cakes. Where did you come from? If that isn't the most concocted idea."

"The same place you did, Detroit. Listen. We can't look suspicious by drawing attention to ourselves, but we have to spy on them. We'll keep on the move. When they are not looking, we'll talk, undercover like."

"Under what cover? I like that part."

"Pay attention. We'll send them distractions to separate them. That's when we can strike up a conversation. You with Debbie and me with Stewart."

"And? I need more than information, dearie. I won't go into the last conversation I had with Debbie."

"We'll spread some nasty rumors about the other person, or something. I haven't worked out all the details."

"Here we go again."

"Do you have a better plan? Or are you just going to let them enjoy Tybee Island together without us?"

"On second thought, okay, pumpkin."

"One more thing. We've got to have a secret 'all clear' sign that we give each other from a distance so that we know that it is okay to approach them."

"What's that?"

"We'll take one shoe off, as a sign."

"I don't know how to explain this to you, honey, but we'll be on the beach. We may already have both of our shoes off."

"Then we'll put one shoe on, if we're not wearing any shoes."

Ralph and Gloria arrived at the beach.

"There's Debbie and Stewart. Let's do it," she said.

"Here? Now?" Ralph joked as he walked away from Gloria.

The pets were having a great time. Some of the dogs were playing Frisbee. Some pets were having their paws printed on construction paper as a souvenir for their owner. Another dog was dancing to the music. Some horses were doing the hustle steps. In a contest, the pigs rolled a ball down a lane with their snouts. The pig that got the ball to the end first, won. The cats were in a jumping contest to see who could leap the furthest over the sand from the start line. The rabbits raced to see which rabbit could run the fastest down the court. Monkeys ran in a short relay game between them and their owners. Dogs were swimming in the portable pet pool in a contest for who could swim the fastest lap.

Debbie entered Butter in the "jump through hoops" contest. Butter learned very quickly and won the contest. Bread won the dog biscuit eating contest.

"Excuse me, sir. Is your name Stewart?" the beach waiter asked.

"Yes." Stewart had a puzzled look on his face.

"There's a call for you at the restaurant, up the beach," the waiter explained.

"That's strange," Stewart said to Debbie. "I'll be right back. Can you watch Bread while I go see who is calling me?"

"I guess, of course," she said as she received Bread's leash from his hand.

Watching from a distance, Gloria, who had decided to wear flip-flops, took off one of her shoes as a sign to Ralph, that all was clear for him to approach Debbie.

Ralph walked by Debbie and then turned around.

"Hi, Debbie. Imagine bumping into you on such a large beach."

Debbie replied cautiously, "Hi, Ralph."

Ralph had two soft drinks in his hand.

"It's kind of hot out here. Have one?"

"No thank you," Debbie said impatiently looking in the direction that Stewart walked. He was inside the restaurant now and out of her sight.

"Where's your friend?" Ralph asked, slightly shaking.

"Stewart went to get a phone call. I can't imagine who would be calling him on the beach during his vacation."

"You can't? It's probably his wife."

"Wife? He said that he wasn't married."

"That's what they all say, doll. Who else would be calling him here on the beach? Think about it. She's probably here in Savannah. Has he invited you to his room?"

"No. I wouldn't have gone, even if he did."

"Doesn't matter. Any decent guy would have at least made the offer, just to see if he was with a decent lady. It's called feeling the chick out, no disrespect."

"I don't think that's true," Debbie looked over to the restaurant to see if Stewart were returning soon.

"Somebody called him, and it's not his Mama. Don't tell him I told you this. Some guys get violent when the truth comes out. I wouldn't want anything to happen to you."

"I never thought of Stewart that way."

"You never know about that kind of person. One minute they are mister nice guy and the next minute mister mean."

Debbie started to tense up. She took a deep breath and tightened her fists.

Bread started jumping up on Ralph. Butter followed Bread.

"Bread and Butter, be nice," Debbie warned them, surprised at their behavior.

"I'm available, anytime, anyplace, if you get into any trouble with this guy. You know I'm not married because we live together; I mean in the same apartment building. I'll protect you because you know you are safe with me," Ralph stammered out, still holding two cups of beverages.

At this point, Bread and Butter started pushing on Ralph harder, causing him to spill both of his beverages.

"Thanks for looking out for me. You are the only person I really know here. I'll think about what you said," Debbie said, confused.

By this time, Bread and Butter knocked the cups right out of Ralph's hands.

"I'm sorry for their behavior, Ralph." Debbie held Bread and Butter back from Ralph.

"I've got to go. See you later." Ralph left.

Back at the restaurant, Stewart asked, "Excuse me, sir. Where is the phone where I have a call waiting for me? I'm Stewart."

"Right over there, sir." The waiter pointed at a phone booth in the corner.

Stewart picked up the phone that was still off the hook.

"Hello?"

Gloria said in a disguised deep husky voice, "Hello. Is that you, Stanley?"

"Stanley? No. I'm Stewart."

"I'm sorry. They went and got the wrong person for me. Please excuse the inconvenience." She hung up the phone.

"That explains it. Wrong number," Stewart said to the waiter on his way out.

Just as he was leaving the restaurant to return to Debbie, Gloria came up to him.

"Hi Stewart. How's it going?" she asked.

"Fine." Stewart kept walking.

"Can I ask you a quick question? Since you're the only person I know here to ask?"

Stewart stopped. "What's the question, Gloria?"

"I don't know how to put this, but that woman you've been seeing. How much do you know about her?"

"Who Debbie? She's a very nice and lovely lady. Why? Do you know something else?"

"As a matter of fact, I do. Promise not to tell anyone

who you got this information from."

"What is it, Gloria?"

"I think I saw her talking to her boyfriend. Whenever you aren't around, he's around."

"What boyfriend? I haven't seen her with anyone but me," Stewart questioned Gloria.

"Have you been with her every minute?"

"No."

"Have you been in her room?"

"Of course not."

"Right, of course not, because maybe she has a boyfriend?"

"Who is he? What's his name? I'll just ask her."

"You can't ask her if she has a boyfriend. She'll only deny it. Then you still won't know."

"Then how will I find out?"

"I'll look out for you. When I see them together again, or find out more, I'll let you know."

"Gloria, please let me know so I can get to the bottom of this. I really appreciate the information. Thanks. You're all right," Stewart gratefully smiled at her.

Gloria caught Ralph out of the corner of her eye, returning to the restaurant. "I think you'd better get back to Debbie before she gets suspicious," she said to Stewart.

"See you later."

"Maybe we can get together before the week is out, so that I can let you know what I find out."

"That's possible." Stewart left the restaurant just before Ralph arrived.

"How did it go?" Ralph asked Gloria.

"Great. How did yours go?"

"Terrific. I think we may be able to pull this off."

"Yeah. We've got to stay out of their sight for the rest of the afternoon, while our plan works."

"I hear there's a Tybee Island Marine Science Center nearby. Want to check it out?" Ralph suggested.

"Sounds good to me. I could use a break from this hot sun. Let's go."

Stewart returned to Debbie. "It was a wrong number."

"Oh, I see," Debbie said in a low voice.

"Anything happen while I was gone?"

"Not much." Debbie dodged the question. "This sun is pretty hot." She looked at a shaded spot by some tall bushes and beach lounging chairs equipped with a side end table.

Debbie pointed. "This looks like a nice spot, and I think the food is free for hotel guests."

"Waiter. Over here please," Stewart motioned with his hands.

They sat back and relaxed, while waiting for their food to arrive. The other pets and their owners were playing from a distance.

Debbie couldn't stop thinking about what Ralph had said.

She wanted to confront Stewart about the subject, but didn't know how to bring it up.

Debbie and Stewart continued to sip on some refreshing fruit beverages. No words were spoken. They glanced at each other and smiled, and then returned to sipping their beverages.

19

Hiding behind some large bushes at the beach on Tybee Island were two young men in their early twenties. They were identical twin brothers named Rob and Bob, dressed in the hotel's pet sitter uniforms.

Abby went from guest to guest asking, "Is everything all right? Comfortable? Where is Peppy, your toy poodle?" Abby asked of one of the guests.

"Your pet sitters came by and offered to take her to relieve herself." The guest explained.

"That's odd. Pet sitter? We don't have any of our pet sitters assigned to the beach party. Which way did they go?" Abby asked with concern.

"Did you say that your pet sitters are not here?" another concerned guest asked.

"That's right. Where is Tabby, your cat?" Abby inquired of her pet.

"A guy in your hotel uniform said he would just take her to the litter box and come right back. That was fifteen minutes ago."

Butter watched Stewart and Debbie sip on their beverages. She crept behind some large bushes nearby to relieve herself. Rob and Bob spotted Butter behind the bushes, alone.

"Look at that yellow cat. This is so easy. Grab it," Rob whispered to Bob.

"This is the last one. We've got a van full already," Bob said.

Rob and Bob snuck up to Butter and grabbed her. They were only a few feet away from Stewart and Debbie who were on the other side of the bushes. Debbie did not realize that Butter was out of her sight.

Bread walked behind the bushes where Butter went. Bob and Rob ran to the hotel van with Butter under Bob's arm.

Bread started running to the van.

Butter meowed loud.

A billy goat was also kidnapped.

Abby ran over in the direction that the guests said the uniformed guys went. Just as she got to the parking lot, she saw the two imposters, Rob and Bob, who were in the stolen hotel van rounding up an assortment of pets from the beach party.

Bread ran up to the door of the van.

"What do you know? A chocolate Lab. We'll take you too, buddy," Rob watched Bread jump into the van where Butter was captured.

"A lab dog. More money."

The brief delay was just enough time for Abby to make it to the van.

"Where are you going with those pets?" Abby shouted.

"Stop right now, or else I'll call the police," she warned the thieves.

"Grab the broad, quick. She can identify us. Tie her up in the van," Rob told Bob.

Bob grabbed Abby and tied her hands and feet with

ropes.

He left her in the cabin of the van with the pets.

"It's done. Let's get out of here," Bob sped down the road to the highway.

By this time Stewart called, "Bread, Bread, where are you?"

"Butter, come here Butter," Debbie shouted with alarm.

"That's strange. They were just here, sitting with us a minute ago. I don't see them anywhere," a visibly upset Debbie cried out.

"They've got to be around. They couldn't just disappear," he assured Debbie. They walked over to the other hotel guests where the pet games had stopped.

The guests started to gather in a cluster. Many of their pets were gone too.

"What's going on?" Stewart asked. "Have you seen Bread, my dog?"

"And Butter, my cat?" Debbie added.

"They took them and my pig and some other pets too," one hotel guest explained.

"What! Where did they go?" an alarmed Stewart asked.

"That's what we want to know," said another irate hotel guest.

"Where's Abby?" Debbie asked in an almost panicked state.

The thieves sped down the highway. Abby was able to see that they had captured at least thirteen pets of all sizes, making the van somewhat crowded.

Abby thought out loud, "What are they going to do with these pets? What will the owners think?" She tried to move and get free of the ropes, but they were tied too tightly for her to loosen them. She also tried to move from her spot, but the thieves had also secured her rope closely to the side of the van's wall. The pets were visibly shaken and frightened. They sensed something was not right.

Back at the beach party, the guests were in an uproar. David arrived after getting a call that something was wrong.

"How could you let this happen?" one guest screamed at him.

"They've got Butter. Do something," Debbie shouted.

"And Bread too," Stewart added.

"Tabby's gone just like that. At a place that's supposed to take care of pets," still another guest scolded.

"Where is Abby?" David asked.

"She's gone too. Someone saw the thieves grab her into the van just before they sped off," one helpful guest explained.

"What! They kidnapped my wife and the pets too?" David fell to his knees.

"It's all your fault. If you had been here, this never would have happened," cried out another guest.

"I have a mind to drag you in that ocean and drown you," one burly man shouted whose pig, Oinky, had been taken.

"I'll help you," shouted another.

Still on his knees, David prayed silently to God, "What shall I do?"

After a moment, David got up off of his knees and called the police on his cellular telephone.

"It's about time you called the police," shouted one irate guest.

"Hurry, please. They might be getting too far away," one very worried guest said.

"This hurts so bad, God. What's going to happen?" David prayed again. "I'm trying to trust You, but this doesn't look good."

"David, is there something we can do?" Stewart asked.

"Trust Him above." David looked up to the heavens.

"We will," Debbie assured David.

David wiped the tears from his eyes. As soon as he turned around, the police arrived.

After getting some information, Lieutenant Cornelius told David, "The scout car is over here. You can ride with us, so that you can identify the van and pets and your wife, of course.

We are doing everything we can to catch them before anything happens."

Once out of David's earshot, Debbie turned to Stewart.

"How could this happen? I thought this was going to be a safe and quiet vacation for Butter and me," an angry Debbie complained to Stewart.

"It just goes to show you that you can't trust anybody," Stewart reflexively blurted out.

Touching a raw nerve, Debbie instinctively said,

"That's right. I'll never trust anyone again with my Butter, anything I have, or my heart."

"What do you mean by that? Your heart? You're the one that's sneaking around my back," Stewart huffed.

"Me? I don't have a wife like you," Debbie shot back.

"Wife? I'm not married."

"That's what they all say. Somebody called you on the phone. It sure wasn't me."

"It was the wrong number."

"That's a good one. Do you expect me to believe such a lame explanation?" Debbie yelled.

"Of course I do. While we are on the subject of explanations, I want to know why you didn't open the door to your room.

Who were you hiding in there?"

"Nobody," Debbie vigorously defended herself.

"Right. How am I supposed to believe that?"

"I could show you the room, but I won't. You'll just have to trust me. I can't go through life defending my every action."

"Neither can I," Stewart fought back.

Back on the van, which was quite a ways down the highway. The younger puppies and kittens started to cry.

"Shut up back there," Bob yelled.

Abby noticed that Bread was looking for a way out of this mess too. She called him over to her.

"Hi, Bread. Look over there. See that red button on the opposite side of the van?

Bread looked in that direction and saw three buttons.

Debbie continued pointing at the red button?

Bread looked over to the buttons.

Butter moved away from the buttons.

Back on the beach, Stewart continued his sparring with Debbie.

"Debbie, in my business, I have to be very careful about whom I can trust, or else I'll get burned along with my client. I'm a lawyer, remember, I get paid to be suspicious."

"Stewart, I'm not your opponent, but if that's the way you see us, then I don't want to be around you."

"That's fine with me. It will make my life a lot simpler."

"Where is Butter? Is there any safe place on earth?" Debbie looked all around, without moving from her spot.

"Are you saying you're not safe with me? That's your problem, you're always going around afraid of everything."

"Afraid? I'm not afraid of you. I just don't trust you."

"Where is Bread? At least he doesn't question my loyalty."

Stewart looked all around, without moving from his spot.

"That's your problem. You expect loyalty, but you don't give it."

Back on the van, "Go ahead, Bread. Push the red button with your paw," Abby coaxed.

Bread went over to the other wall of the van. He pushed the blue button. Just then, the lights flashed and the horn started blowing. Soft elevator music played throughout the speakers in the van, soothing the pets. Soft pastel lights came on, further calming the pets.

"Not the blue one, Bread. You pushed the wrong button," Abby said.

"Where did that music and light come from? Who told you to turn on the lights, blow the horn and play music?" an angry Bob scolded Rob.

"I didn't do anything," Rob shrugged his shoulders and scratched his head.

The thieves knocked on the back panel of the van connecting the passenger cabin.

"I said be quiet in there, or I'm coming back there to make you permanently quiet."

"Hurry Bread. Push the other button, the red one on the right," Abby encouraged Bread to try again.

He proceeded to push the read button with his right paw.

Nothing happened. The pets started shaking more.

"Shush, little ones, help is on the way. If the police reach us before we leave this van, we'll be okay," Abby said.

Back at the beach, "Debbie, if you want to be with your boyfriend instead of me, just be open about it. Don't string me along or play with my heart," Stewart said.

"Stewart, I don't have a boyfriend and don't intend on having one soon, especially when they've got a wife."

"I don't have a wife or a girlfriend. You don't have to

20

"Lieutenant, we've got a signal!" The police officer called to the police command station.

"The van is traveling on Highway 111 leading to the produce loading dock at the pier."

"Let's go!" Lt. Cornelius ordered.

"Calling all police squad cars in the vicinity of the produce pier. Be on the lookout for a white van labeled 'Pets-by-the-Sea Hotel.' Set up a barricade on Slaughter Street near the pier. Stop all vans."

The lieutenant, with David in the car, sped off to the pier. The sirens turned on as they headed down Highway 111.

A police officer at the beach announced to the guests, "They've located the van. Let's all go back to the hotel and wait for further information. The hotel is sending some vans to take you back."

"I'm not riding in the same van with you," Debbie told Stewart.

"Fine." Stewart boarded a different van.

Back on the van, "We are going to get out of this dilemma somehow. You'll all be back with your owners soon." Abby's words of comfort seemed to calm the baby pets down.

The van stopped at the produce pier.

"It's time to make the switch, Bob. What are we

going to do with the woman?" Rob asked Bob.

"I don't know. We've got to take her with us or else she can finger what you look like to the cops."

"Remember, if she identifies your face, she's identified mine too," Rob pointed out to his identical twin.

"I forgot."

"Let's move fast. We don't have much time." Bob dashed to the back doors of the van.

Abby told the pets, "When they open that door, stay close to me. We all have to stay together and not leave the van to be safe. Someone is on the way."

Bread and Butter acted like sheep dogs as they coaxed the pets to huddle in the back of the van by Abby. Bread and Butter faced the van's door as they stood in front of the pets and Abby.

"Bark! Bark! Bark! Meow! Meow! Meow!" protectively went Bread and Butter as the doors of the van opened.

"I told you we should have tied them up first," Rob complained to Bob.

The sound of sirens pierced the air. The sirens got louder.

"We're busted. How dumb can you get trying to steal pets?" Bob asked to Rob.

"I'm as smart as you are," Rob reminded Bob.

"Turn around with your hands up," the policeman shouted through the bullhorn.

"How did they find us so fast?" Bob said in puzzlement.

"Who cares? How am I going to explain this to Mom, that her sons are in jail for stealing kittens?"

A police officer opened the van doors wider. The pets leaped for joy and some literally into the arms of the police officers.

"There, there buddy. Everything is going to be all right," one officer assured a trembling puppy.

"You're a cute kitten. We'll get you back to your owner in just a little while," another officer comforted a shaken kitten.

Bread and Butter started jumping around in joy.

"Okay, let's get these pets back to their owners," Lt. Cornelius directed his officers.

Butter lingered for a moment in the van. She pushed the third OnTime white button with her paw. She jumped when a voice on the speaker asked, "Hello, this is your OnTime operator. May I help you?"

Butter ran out of the van as quickly as she could, jumping into the arms of Lt. Cornelius.

"Everything is fine, operator," Abby replied into the speaker.

"We're safe and okay,"

"Very good. Have a nice evening,"

The police placed all the animals in squad cars and rescue vans to be returned to the hotel.

David eagerly walked over to the van, looked inside, and there was Abby, tied up but otherwise unharmed.

He leaped into the van, hugged his wife, and asked, "Are you all right?"

"I couldn't be better, now that you're here," Abby gleefully smiled. "But there is one thing you could do for me, dear."

"Anything. What is it?"

"Untie me please." Abby looked in the direction of the ropes that were still around her wrists and ankles.

"Of course. Right now," David sheepishly replied.

They both emerged together from the van.

Lt. Cornelius asked Abby, "Are you okay?"

"Yes. I'm fine."

"Would you mind stepping over here for a moment while we ask you some questions about the kidnapping?"

"I'd be happy to," she said. "If it weren't for Bread, we wouldn't have made it out alive. He saved our lives by pushing the OnTime button, allowing you to track us."

While David was waiting for his wife to finish with the police, he noticed the two thieves, handcuffed in the scout car. Suddenly he ran over and pounded on the window, trying to open the locked door. "I'll get you for this. No one treats my wife like that." His temper flared hotter and hotter. The other officers attempted to restrain him from attacking the suspects.

Abby saw the commotion and ran over to her husband. "The police have them. They will see justice. Let the police handle it. Please stop, honey," Abby pleaded with her husband.

"Don't do anything you will regret later. Think of the hotel and pets. Think of our son, Timothy, too. What was the Bible lesson you taught this morning?"

"It was on forgiveness. That's got nothing to do with this situation."

"When did you say to forgive?"

"Okay, let's drop the subject. Are you sure you're

not hurt?" David asked.

"I'm fine. Everyone's fine."

David went over to a bench and sat down. Abby rubbed his back to cool him down.

Lt. Cornelius directed the police officer, "Get these suspects to the police station for further processing." He then turned to David and Abby. "I'll drive you and your wife back to the hotel. We've sent word out for the pet owners to meet us there.

Ready?'"

"I'm ready," David replied.

While riding back to the hotel, Abby asked David, "Are you hungry? I bet you haven't eaten dinner yet."

"I am a little."

"I'll call ahead, to ask our chef to make up a nice carry out meal."

Since the episode made TV news coverage, the citizens of Savannah were lined up along the streets leading back to the hotel, waving their hands at the cavalcade of about ten police vehicles passing by. It looked like a parade. Some of the citizens clapped and cheered.

Upon checking for fingerprints on the OnTime button, the police officer radioed back to Lt. Cornelius, "It looks like a large dog's paw pushed the button. We've got a hero."

"Isn't he the same dog that rescued the cat on our boat's tour Monday?" David asked Abby.

"He sure is. He is a hero twice."

As soon as they got to the hotel, Lt. Cornelius went over to the scout car where Bread was located.

"Congratulations, again! Someone ought to write a book about you," Lt. Cornelius joked.

Debbie and Stewart rushed out of the hotel lobby to opposite sides of the front yard to retrieve their pets. Also waiting at the entrance were TV camerapersons and news reporters, hovering around Bread, the hero.

Butter saw Stewart first, and led the officer to him.

"Is this your cat?" the officer asked Stewart.

"No."

"Can you direct me to the owner?"

Just then, Debbie saw Bread first and approached him as the TV cameramen and reporters surrounded him.

"Is this your dog?" the reporter asked.

"No."

"Where is his owner?"

Before she could answer, Stewart approached Bread with Butter being carried by the officer. Butter leaped out of the officer's arms to get to Bread. Bread and Butter started jumping around in excitement. Their leashes intertwined with each other.

"Good dog!" Stewart shouted as he hugged Bread. "Want some bread biscuits?"

Bread waved this tail vigorously.

"Butter, my pure Butter." Debbie reached out her arms to pick Butter up.

"I'll never leave you, Butter. What an ordeal you've been through. What a strong and brave cat too." Debbie hugged Butter.

Butter purred at Debbie's strokes.

As Debbie and Stewart started to walk away with their pets, the leashes got more tangled.

"How did you get tangled up so fast? Let me try this," Debbie said to Butter.

"That's not going to work. It's only getting more entangled." Stewart continued to try to unravel the mess. As they both struggled to untangle the leashes, their hands accidentally touched. As they stooped down closer to their pets, their faces almost touched.

Her hair brushed up against his cheek. Stewart looked at Debbie, and she returned the gaze. As Bread and Butter continued to playfully cajole each other, Debbie wasn't watching what she was doing and got her foot entangled in Butter's leash, throwing her off balance. She fell into Stewart's arms as he instinctively caught her to keep her from falling to the ground.

"Excuse me. Sorry about that," she apologized.

"No, that was all right," he responded.

For a moment, she stayed in his arms. They both rose up and continued to unravel the last tangled part of the leases. Finally, they got the leashes untangled.

"Come on Bread, we need to be alone," Stewart said to Bread.

"Come on Butter, let's leave." Bread and Butter just sat there not budging.

"I guess they're tired," Stewart surmised.

"They've been through a lot today. They probably just want to rest for a moment," Debbie reasoned.

"Yeah. Debbie, do you think maybe we could rest a little too?' he sat down at a bench nearby.

"I guess so." she sat down with him.

"If you don't believe anything else about me, know that if I had a woman in my life, she would be you," he said.

"How am I supposed to know if I can believe what you say?" Debbie asked emotionally drained and exasperated.

He paused. "You'll have to go by what's inside here." He gently took her hand and placed it over his heart.

"Stewart." She took his other hand into hers and sat, savoring the moment.

She concluded, "I guess we'll both have to trust the Holy Spirit to guide us."

"In my heart, there is no one but you." Their eyes met again.

"I know."

The four of them were all together again.

"Trust the Lord," Stewart began.

"In all thy ways," Debbie continued.

Bread and Butter just rested on their paws.

The beach party was over. The owners finished talking to the police and returned to their rooms for rest, after a very exhausting day. However, there was one photographer who took pictures of the abandoned beach party grounds, where the guest's belongings were strewn all over the beach. In their hurry to reunite with their pets, the beach litter was left. The photographer mumbled, "This will show them."

Ralph and Gloria had visited the Beach Science Center the greater part of the afternoon to stay cool and out of sight. By the time they left the Center, all the hotel guests had left. They missed all of the commotion from the kidnapping and rescue.

"Where did everyone go?" she asked him.

"I don't even see the van. Let's take a cab."

While riding back in the cab, Ralph said, "I've got to make a call."

"Me too. Debbie and Stewart are probably feeling so jilted that they will practically run into our arms for comfort."

Ralph called Debbie.

"Hello?" Debbie answered the telephone.

"Hi Debbie. It's Ralph. Can I take you out for an exciting evening and dinner?"

"That's nice of you to ask, but I've had enough excitement for one day. I'm very tired. By the way, Stewart and I have decided to trust each other. I'm glad your conversation with me allowed me to open up the topic with him. Thanks."

"You're welcome." Ralph halfheartedly replied.

Gloria called Stewart.

"Hello," Stewart answered the telephone.

"Hi Stewart. It's Gloria. I was wondering if we could meet at the restaurant tonight for a small evening snack, maybe chat a little."

"Not tonight. I'm exhausted. I just want to spend a little time with Bread."

"I understand. How are things going with you and Debbie?"

Gloria asked, nervously twirling her hair around her right finger.

"It's nice of you to ask. We had a heart-to-heart talk about trust. We're closer than ever. Emotions aren't always bad, if you just lay them out on the table and deal with them, honestly and sincerely. I have you to thank for that."

"Don't mention it," Gloria said flatly.

Everyone was exhausted. The evening turned out to be a quiet night, with all resting up for tomorrow.

21

"Good morning. Front desk."

"Hi Martha. This is Gloria. I see on the Thursday schedule today that there is a Pet Talent Show this afternoon. Rehearsals are this morning. I'd like to rehearse for the Pet Talent Show with my Goldies in the same room where Bread will be. Is that possible?"

"You and a lot of people want to be in the same room with Bread. He's a very popular pet. However, I think I can squeeze in a few goldfish. That's conference room A."

"Thanks. Can you also put Talker in the other room with Butter?"

"Sure, that will be in conference room B."

"Great. We'll be there at 10:00 a.m."

Gloria dialed Ralph's room. "Hello Ralph."

"This better be good. It's 9:00 a.m., doll," half-awake Ralph said.

"All we have to do to win Debbie and Stewart over is be nice to their pets. You help Debbie rehearse with Butter. I'll help Stewart rehearse with Bread. They'll see how well we get along with their pets. That way they can't help but love us."

"Hmm, not bad. How difficult can it be to get along with a cat named Butter?"

"Right. Bread should be a piece of cake too."

"Okay. You're on, snookems."

Debbie and Butter were getting ready to go to rehearsal.

"I'll always be with you," Debbie comforted Butter.

Butter squirmed from the coziness.

Debbie arrived in conference room B, where the cats and the smaller pets rehearsed.

The hotel placed the dogs and larger animals in conference room A for rehearsal.

Ralph approached Debbie.

"Did you know that I've been around a lot of chicks, I mean kittens, or cats in my lifetime?" Ralph began.

"No. I didn't."

"What kind of talent is Butter going to do?"

"I haven't thought much about it."

"I'm sure with her personality she should be good at anything we teach her. Take Butter here. You and Butter have a great relationship right?"

"Of course."

"All you need is a few lines, I mean techniques, and she will be performing like a star. May I show you, Debbie?"

"Okay. But don't hurt her."

"I wouldn't think of it," Ralph reached over to pat Butter.

Butter hissed. She took a swipe at him. He moved his hand away quickly before she connected.

"Easy, kitty, easy. Why don't I stand right over here and give you a few pointers, at least until Butter warms up to me a little more. I can tell that she likes me though."

"You think so?"

Butter's back rose up while looking straight at Ralph. Ralph stepped back.

"Just tie a string around some cat food and watch her go wherever you like by pulling the food around and dangling it."

"Like this?" Debbie tied a fish shaped cat food nugget on a string. Butter pushed a 6-inch plastic red ball around in a circle by chasing the food nugget.

"Right. Like that. We can't, I mean you can't lose, doll."

Ralph smiled at Debbie.

Gloria was befriending Bread in the other room.

"Hi Stewart. I'm really good with animals. Mind if I help you with Bread's rehearsal?"

"Hi Gloria. No. I don't mind, especially since I've never done this before."

"What are you trying to teach him?"

"Just some simple dog tricks."

Bread looked away from Gloria.

"See? All you have to do is ask him to turn around in a circle on his hind feet, then reward him with a dog treat."

When the dog treat appeared, he did exactly what he was shown to do.

"Bread, you are doing great!" Gloria patted him on the head before giving him another treat.

"Gee, Gloria, I didn't know you were so good with

animals. I'm really impressed," Stewart smiled.

"It really comes easy for me. Bread and I get along real well."

"It's almost 12 noon. We'd better grab lunch before the 2:00 p.m. Talent Show," Stewart noted.

"Sounds good to me," Gloria smiled.

"Welcome to the Pet Talent Show, where pets get to show off a little," David announced.

"Hi, Debbie. Ready for the Talent Show?" Stewart asked.

"Yes. Where shall we sit?" Debbie replied.

"I like the front. I see two seats up there."

"Great."

"How did it go?" Gloria asked Ralph in the back of the room.

"We're making progress." Ralph replied.

"Good. We should not sit together. I'll sit on one side of the room and you can sit on the other." Gloria kept an eye on Debbie and Stewart who were now seated up front.

"Okay, sweetheart." Ralph sat with Talker in the back, opposite from Gloria.

"Our first act is a monkey riding a bike," David announced.

"Let's give an applause for the monkey."

The audience clapped.

"Our next act is from Butter."

Butter performed perfectly by pushing the red ball around in a circle with her feet and nose.

"Wasn't she brilliant?" David noted.

The audience clapped.

"Next we have Bread," he announced.

Bread stood on his hind feet and turned around in circles at Stewart's prompt and for the dog treat.

"Great performance, Bread." David applauded.

The audience clapped.

"Our next act is by Talker."

"Oh boy! I was so busy teaching Butter a routine, I forgot to teach Talker one," Ralph said to himself.

"Here comes Talker," David repeated.

Ralph began, "What's the difference between an elephant and a giraffe?"

Talker just sat in his cage without saying a word.

Ralph cleared his voice and continued with another joke.

"Why did the chicken lay an egg?"

Ralph looked at Talker, who said nothing at all.

Ralph in irritation demanded, "Say something, anything, after all. Why do you think they call you Talker?"

"Ask the jerk that called me Talker. I don't know. I'm a parakeet," Talker responded.

Everyone laughed, except Ralph. His image was tarnished.

He was supposed to look good, not bad. As Ralph returned to his seat, he took a look at Debbie who was laughing at him with the rest of the audience.

"This is so embarrassing," Ralph mumbled as he

lowered his head.

"Let us now welcome the Goldies," David announced.

Gloria stood and went to the front. She wore a metallic gold embroidered costume in the shape of a goldfish. It was sleeveless and legless, almost like a bathing suit, only padded in extended areas for fins.

"My Goldies are going to sing 'I Just Want to Be with You' karaoke style," Gloria explained.

Gloria placed the goldfish on a gold metallic tablecloth that covered a small round lamp table. She turned on the audiotape for background music. She hid under the table with a remote microphone. She sung from under the table while the Goldies swam in the fishbowl on the top of the table.

Gloria's beautiful voice sung,

I just want to be with you.

Be with you.

Be with you.

I just want to hold your hand,

Hold your hand.

Hold your hand.

I'll be with you through and through.

Through and through.

Through and through.

I just want you to be my man.

Be my man.

Be my man.

"Let's give a big hand of applause for the Goldies."

172

David and the audience clapped in approval.

Gloria attempted to get up from behind the small table to take a bow with the Goldies. Her goldfish costume caught on the tablecloth. As she struggled to pull away from the snare, the fishbowl with the Goldies started to slide off the now slanted tabletop. She reached for the fishbowl, which caused the table to tip further. The fishbowl fell to the floor. There was a mad rush by some of the cats and birds to get to the fish to eat them. Gloria dashed over the top of the table to retrieve the Goldies and the table collapsed. She quickly grabbed the fish by her hands just in time to save them. There she was, flat on her stomach, torn goldfish costume, over a fallen table with the Goldies barely swimming in the shallow water remaining.

"That was some encore!" David chuckled.

The whole audience laughed at her, including Stewart.

Gloria's face turned red in humiliation. She ran out of the room in tears.

"That's an act we won't forget," David commented.

Ralph left the room to find Gloria. He found her in the Pet Chapel, alone in tears with her Goldies.

"Ralph," Gloria sobbed, "I've been trying so hard to make this work. All I do is fall on my face."

"Literally," Ralph joked before he caught himself. "I think we both felt like idiots. Anyway, they thought it was just part of the act," Ralph countered himself on a more serious note.

"Look at me. What was I trying to prove by looking like a goldfish? I'm a complete failure. I'm nothing. That's what I am," Gloria sobbed uncontrollably.

"I wouldn't go that far. In fact, you're not a failure at all."

"I'm not?"

Ralph took her face in his hands, and looked through all the smeared mascara, smudged lipstick and goldfish costume.

"It's what's inside that counts. You have a heart of gold for even trying so hard to get a man to notice you."

"I do?" she looked at him.

"Yes, you do. And you're not bad lookin' either," he nudged her gently on the chin.

"You've been so wonderful throughout this whole thing. Here I am crying over another man, and you're here comforting me." Gloria's sniffles slowed.

"No. I'm not that great."

"Yes, you are. You've gone along with every scheme I've cooked up. It takes a real man to be so concerned about a person that you've known for such a short time."

"Short time?" he reflected. "It seems like I've known you for a lifetime."

"Me too."

Ralph put his arms around Gloria as she rested her head on his shoulders, while sitting there in the quiet stillness of the Pet's Chapel.

Just then, David opened the door. Slightly embarrassed, they pretended to smooth their clothes and moved apart. But a bond had been formed that neither could deny.

"I just came to see if everyone was okay. I was concerned when you did not return to the room for the rest of the Talent Show."

Ralph stood up. "Yes, we're fine."

"I had to get some more water for the Goldies," Gloria explained as she stood up to straighten her outfit.

David looked at the goldfish that were still swimming in very tight waters.

"And I had to take Talker to church to teach him some manners," Ralph explained, standing with Talker twenty feet away in his cage.

"I see." David smiled and left the Chapel with the two of them standing there.

"He didn't believe a word we said," Ralph laughed.

"That was kind of funny. Us two in the Chapel and all," she laughed.

"I guess we'd better go back for the rest of the Talent Show."

Ralph opened the door for Gloria.

"I really don't feel like going back." Gloria said with a somber sigh.

"Neither do I."

"I think I'll just go back to the hotel room and relax for the rest of the evening,"

"I'll walk you to your room, just to make sure you're all right."

"Thanks. I'd like that."

The Talent Show was over. The guests gathered their things and pets to leave the room. A stranger came up to David with a paper in his hand and gave it to him without saying a word before he walked away. David read the paper. His countenance quickly went from cheerfulness to sadness. Abby joined him.

They both looked down at the paper. Debbie noticed that David's head was bowed as he and Abby sat down in a corner of the room. She and Stewart went over to them.

"What's the matter?" she asked.

"The 'People Against Pets' have filed a petition with the court to ban pets from hotels," David replied.

"Why?" Stewart asked.

"They say we are disturbing the peace and are a nuisance. It is really because they want our land. They are trying to do it under the guise that our pet guests are ruining their business and the neighborhood."

"That can't be true," Debbie said in shock.

"I know. This property has been in our family for seventy years, long before this area was built up. We are now sitting on the most valuable real estate in Savannah, not to mention the county. It used to be an animal-breeding farm. It has evolved over the years into this lovely, friendly place. In fact, the animals were here before these commercial developers. We take great pride in being neat, clean, and neighborly," David said indignantly.

"You're going to fight it, aren't you?" Debbie asked with great concern.

"I want to, but I don't know how. They have the best lawyer in the country."

"Who is that?" Stewart asked.

"Lena Wynns."

"Good luck. I'm glad I'm not going up against her. She's known for being tough all right."

"I can't find any local attorneys willing to take the case. They say they don't want to go up against those folks," David lamented.

"I'm sure you'll do well. I'm sure everything's in order," Stewart stepped away about to leave.

Abby joined in the conversation. "The city inspected the place last week and issued us a clean bill of health. Nevertheless, the neighbors, who are all hotel owners too, won't drop the lawsuit to have us shut down."

Debbie looked at Stewart.

"What I will do is pray for you," he said.

"Stewart, they need more than prayers. They need you," Debbie said looking into his eyes.

"Me?" Stewart resisted.

"Yes, you. You're a lawyer," she reminded him.

"You are a lawyer?" David said with surprise.

"Please help the pets. This is the only place in America that has a hotel devoted to combined pets' and owners' activities," Abby pleaded.

"I'd like to but, if you haven't noticed, I'm on vacation. Remember? I paid $10,000 to do nothing," he objected.

"Stewart, that's a lame excuse. If it wasn't for this hotel, you and Bread wouldn't have had this vacation," Debbie argued.

"I would, but there just isn't enough time. I'm sure you can get a continuance for more time to find the right lawyer."

"This is a rescheduled hearing because the last lawyer dropped the case. That was the confirmation paper I just received," David explained.

"Then why don't you get someone else?"

"I told you, or maybe I didn't, I'm so confused right now. I can't find anyone locally to take on the local merchants. Besides, I need an attorney to go up against someone like Lena Wynns."

"I won't be in town. I'm leaving Saturday," Stewart dodged. "No problem. The hearing is tomorrow, Friday." Abby said with anticipation.

"What! You want me to prepare for your case and present it before the judge and against Lena Wynns by tomorrow?"

"Come on, Stewart. God is on your side. You can do it," Debbie rallied.

Stewart looked up to the sky, "I appreciate your help Lord. If you don't mind, I'll pass on this one. Thanks anyway. I gratefully decline."

"I don't believe you. I thought you were compassionate, dedicated to justice and an all around good guy. But now I am having second thoughts about your character," Debbie said, eyes stern, lips smiling coyly.

"Do it for God, my son," David asked with praying hands.

"I do want to do the right thing. Give me a moment to think."

There was dead silence, as all eyes fixed on him, waiting for a yes.

He walked over to a nearby table and noticed an open Bible.

He picked up the Bible and there highlighted on the page was First Corinthians 9:24-25: *"Know ye not that they which run in a race run all, but one receiveth the prize? So run, that ye may obtain."*

"I'll agree, but only if you are going to be my assistant," Stewart said to Debbie.

"Me? But I'm not an attorney," she said in surprise.

"You don't have to be an attorney to be my assistant. Between now and tomorrow you'll know everything you want to know about nuisance law and animal law, but were afraid to ask," Stewart joked.

"We can work on it in my hotel room," he said gearing up for a long night.

"No way am I going to be in a hotel guest room with a man. Didn't I tell you that?" Debbie protested.

"We've got a Business Center conference room that has a computer, fax, internet, everything. It has glass windows to the corridor and my staff will be around to assist you with any supplies or food you may need. It even has an area for your pets," Abby facilitated.

"Hear that? We are going to work on this together, or not at all," Stewart demanded.

"When do we start?" Debbie said sheepishly.

"Now."

"Thank you my son and daughter. God will bless you for this. Right this way to the conference room," David beamed with a spring in his step.

In the conference room, Stewart and Debbie plowed through the Internet for legal research, the court pleadings and potential exhibits.

"It's hopeless. Based on these papers and my legal research, this will be a very difficult case to win," Stewart said in exhaustion. He slumped in his chair.

"Nothing is hopeless to God," Debbie piped. "We are

going to win this case. Keep looking."

Abby walked back into the conference room. "I brought you some sandwiches and beverages. How are we looking?"

"Great," Debbie said.

"Not so fast. What we need is more proofs. What else do you have?" Stewart asked.

"We gave you everything we had," David said.

"Then I'll keep looking at them. Maybe I missed something."

"In the meantime, we need to go over your testimony. I'm afraid you are our only witness, David."

"So far," Debbie added.

"Right. We've got all of ten hours to find more witnesses, prep them and have them already to go," Stewart said sarcastically looking at his watch that read 11:00 p.m.

"What do you want me to do next?" Debbie tried to encourage everyone to keep focused.

"Right now? Pray," Stewart suggested.

Bread and Butter were sound asleep in the corner resting on each other like a pillow.

"If only all mankind could live together so peacefully," Debbie said as she glanced over to the pets.

"One day there will be peace on earth," David said.

"But until that moment, get to work guys. We've got a hearing to prepare for." Stewart focused them back to their purpose at hand.

"It's two o'clock in the morning. I'm sleepy," Debbie yawned.

"We've got to get some sleep if we are going to get to a 9:00 a.m. hearing on time," Stewart noted.

"Right," Debbie yawned again.

"Did we get enough to win the case, Stewart?" David asked.

"I don't know. We'll do our best,"

"You've got to win this case. Our pets are counting on you," the obviously exhausted Abby pleaded.

"Get some rest, everybody. That's the best thing we should do at this moment," Stewart instructed them.

"Good night. I'll pick you up in the hotel car at 8:00 a.m."

David and Abby prepared to leave the conference room.

"Good night, my children," David said as he and Abby left the room.

"Come on Butter. Let's go back to our room." Both she and Butter were groggy. She picked Butter up and turned to Stewart. "Regardless of what happens tomorrow, thanks."

"I've never prepared for a case in one day. I usually have a few years' advance notice."

"It'll work out. Sometimes, we just have to put things in God's hands," Debbie assured him.

"That's exactly where we are. Good night. I'll walk you to your room. You don't suppose they'll give me a $10,000 refund for this?"

"Stewart, they've already incurred the expenses of entertaining you this week."

"You're right. Just a thought. If I do win this case against Ms. Wynns, I'll probably be famous."

Debbie laughed. "And you'll have to take another vacation."

"That will cost me more money."

"Good night, Stewart."

"Pleasant dreams, Debbie."

22

"Hello," Debbie groggily answered the telephone.

"It's seven. Time to get up. We've got a big case to win," Stewart chimed.

"Is that a.m. or p.m.?" Debbie joked, half-asleep.

"It's a.m. If you don't get up right now, I'm coming over there to get you up."

"I'm up. I'm up," she said trying to laugh, but too sleepy.

"We can't take Bread and Butter with us to court. Who's going to watch the pets?" he asked.

"What about the Pet Care Center?" she suggested.

"It doesn't open before 9:00 a.m."

"I met a nice lady who is right next door. I'll ask her to watch Butter. What about Bread?"

"I could ask the guy I met. He said that if I ever needed someone to watch my dog, he'd do it. I'll call him right now."

"Great."

Gloria's phone rang.

"Hello," she answered.

"This is Debbie. I know this is short notice, but can you watch my cat, Butter, for the morning? I have to take care of some business downtown."

"Certainly. What time?"

"I'm bringing her over right after I take a shower and get dressed in about 30 minutes?"

"I'll be here."

"Thanks."

"Hello, Ralph? Remember when you said you'd watch my dog?" Stewart asked.

"Yeah. What's up, man." Ralph was only half awake.

"I need a favor. Can you watch him now?"

"Now?"

"As soon as I get dressed."

"Sure. I'll leave the door unlocked. Just bring him in."

"Thanks, Ralph."

"No problem. By the way, what's happening this early in the morning?" Ralph asked.

"It's something important that I have to do down at the courthouse. It shouldn't last long. I'll bring him over in 30 minutes."

"No problem." Ralph rolled back over to sleep.

"It's 7:59 a.m. Where is she?" Stewart asked David.

"Hi everyone. I'm here. Let's go," Debbie breathlessly dashed down the hallway to the lobby.

"The car is right out here. Are we ready?" David escorted them to the car.

"As ready as we are ever going to be." Stewart opened the car door for Debbie.

David drove to the courthouse with Abby by his side, along with Debbie and Stewart.

"This is the place." David pushed the button for the fourth floor where the hearing was to take place.

"Where is the jury?" David whispered to Stewart.

"Apparently your previous counsel agreed to a bench trial where the judge is the jury," Stewart whispered back.

"The case of 'People Against Pets v. Pets-by-the-Sea Hotel,' is now scheduled to be heard," Judge Wright's court clerk announced.

"Who is the counsel for the plaintiff?" Judge Wright began.

Lena Wynns stood to address the court.

"Your Honor, Lena Wynns, on behalf of the People Against Pets."

"Who is the counsel on behalf of the defendant?" the judge asked.

"Your Honor, Stewart Counts, on behalf of the Pets-by-the- Sea Hotel."

"Do you have an opening statement, Ms. Wynns?"

"Yes I do, Your Honor. As we are all aware, this is the 21st century. What was acceptable in the roaring twenties may not be acceptable in the technological twenty-first. People, tourists in particular, come to Savannah to relax, enjoy the scenic views of our well-maintained historic homes and manicured parks. Many come to see the Atlantic Ocean for the very first time. The last thing we want our visitors and citizens to see is frisky unruly dogs and cats running wild through the parks, filthy pigs at the ice cream café and trash strewn all over our pristine beaches from littering pets. Therefore, we ask the court to put an end to this unbridled establishment they call a hotel, for the good of the people. We, the People Against Pets, ask that you declare the Pets-by-the-Sea Hotel to be a nuisance. We further ask this court to immediately shut it down with a permanent injunction and order that all costs and attorney fees be paid by the defendant."

"Thank you, Ms. Wynns. Do you have an opening statement, Mr. Counts?"

"Yes I do, Your Honor."

"The hotel runs a very respectable and efficient operation. The pets are clean, neat and orderly. Therefore, we respectfully request that you deny the plaintiff's request."

"That's it?" Debbie mumbled to Stewart.

"I want to see what they have before I say more than I can prove," Stewart explained.

"Thank you Mr. Counts. The plaintiff may call her first witness."

"I put on as my first witness, Ms. Sue Snipe."

The judge offered the testifying oath to the witness.

"Ms. Snipe, please tell us who you are," Ms. Wynns opened.

"I am a member of the People Against Pets. I am also their photographer."

"Tell us why the People Against Pets filed this petition."

"People were complaining that they kept seeing all kinds of animals running around and birds flying around. There were all kinds of living things that they shouldn't have to be bothered with when people are on a vacation."

"Can you be more specific?"

"Certainly. There are dogs and cats mainly, but also pigs, horses, reptiles, live fish and even birds all over the place. It is all so disgusting. I took these pictures this week to illustrate our point," Ms. Snipe said.

Debbie whispered in Stewart's ear, "She's the photographer we saw all week."

David whispered in Stewart's other ear, "She must have been spying on the hotel. I don't believe they would be so sneaky."

Stewart interrupted the direct examination.

"Excuse me, Your Honor, this is the first time we have heard about the plaintiff having any pictures as evidence. May we see them?"

The judge motioned his hand for Ms. Wynns to show the pictures to Stewart.

"May we have a few minutes to review them?" Stewart asked.

"Very well. Let's take a fifteen minute recess."

Back at the hotel after a few extra winks, Gloria made a call.

"Hello Ralph, it's me, Gloria. I didn't remember seeing anything on the hotel's itinerary for this morning. Did Debbie say anything to you about why she had to leave Butter with me so suddenly?"

"No. It's funny you should ask. Stewart asked me to watch Bread for a short time this morning too."

"That's strange. Where did he say he was going?"

"The courthouse."

"What! The courthouse? Debbie said she had to take care of some business downtown. They must be getting married! What else could they be doing on such a short notice?"

"No. I don't think so."

"I do. We've got to stop them. They're supposed to be marrying us!"

"Hold on, Gloria. Let's not jump to conclusions."

"All right. You explain it, will you?"

"I don't know why they both happen to be going downtown. They probably went in separate cars and had different things to do. It's just a coincidence that it's at the same time." Ralph conjectured.

"Think about it. They are on their vacation. There is no other business to do. Get dressed, Ralph. We need to stop a wedding. I'll meet you in the lobby in twenty minutes."

"I'll be ready, even though I still think you are wrong about this. Men don't up and marry women they just meet, not levelheaded men like Stewart. Besides, Debbie barely lets a man touch her, much less marry her."

"People do strange things when they are in love, Ralph."

"Come to think of it, they sure do."

"Get dressed. I'll see you in fifteen minutes."

"What about their pets? We can't leave them in the room after we said we would look after them."

"We'll have to take them with us," she quickly hung up the phone.

Fifteen minutes later, Ralph and Gloria were in the lobby with Bread and Butter. In her hurry to get dressed, she forgot to comb her hair. She also put on one orange high heel pump and one green high heel pump without realizing it. She wore a scooped neck sleeveless t-shirt, but forgot to pull one of the thin shoulder straps over her shoulder so that her bra strap was showing on the otherwise bare shoulder. She did put on her make-up, but put too much powder on from her loose powder puff. It looked like extra powder here and there on her face and neck and ears.

Ralph, who was still half asleep, didn't seem to notice her disarray.

"Where is the manager? We'd like to use the hotel car,"

Gloria asked at the front desk.

"My dad took the car to the courthouse."

"You mean, your Dad, the minister? Was anyone with him?"

Gloria asked in a panic.

"Yes," Timothy calmly said.

"Was it Stewart and Debbie, by chance?"

"Yes, I believe so."

"Did you hear that?" she said with alarm.

"Is there another car we can use?" Ralph asked, waking up now with the new information.

"All we have available at this time is the hotel station wagon."

"We'll take it," Gloria eagerly replied.

"Which way to the courthouse?" Ralph asked.

Timothy handed Ralph the keys. "The station wagon's out front and the courthouse is just down the road to the left. You can't miss it. Remember, rushing won't make the world go faster," Timothy laughed with his hyena laugh.

Both Gloria and Ralph ran out the door with Bread and Butter in tow on their leashes.

"Did you hear that? They went with the minister to the courthouse to get married." Gloria was visibly upset. "We've got to get there fast, Ralph."

"They're really going to do it," he said in amazement, as he drove off to the courthouse.

Judge Wright announced, "Recess is over. We are now back in court session."

Ms. Wynns resumed her direct examination.

"Ms. Snipe, please tell us about this first snapshot."

"This is a dead pet mouse, just lying there in the lobby, after the front desk clerk, Martha, stomped it to death."

The judge gasped at the lifeless mouse just before giving a stern look over his eyeglass rim at David.

Debbie whispered to Stewart, "It wasn't on a leash. It couldn't have been a pet."

Stewart looked at Debbie in puzzlement.

"This is a picture of a cat nearly drowning in the Atlantic Ocean. This shows how irresponsible the hotel is." Ms. Snipe held up a picture of Butter in the ocean. "This is another picture of the hotel jeopardizing a dog's life because the dog is out there in the ocean too, almost drowning. Is that their idea of fun?" Ms. Snipe sniped.

"Your Honor, please instruct the witness not to ask questions," Stewart objected.

"Ms. Snipe, just answer the questions, please."

"Yes, Your Honor. This picture. You've just got to see it.

"Here is a photograph at their wild beach party of

people dancing with pets on their heads."

"They were just having a little fun," Abby mumbled to Stewart.

"It's an embarrassment to the image of our great city. On that same night, valuable police resources were used to capture a pet thief ring. See the mutt wrapped in company issued blankets? What a waste," Ms Snipe jabbed.

"I object. That mutt is a Labrador retriever." Stewart defended Bread.

"What's the difference? They are a drain on our resources and attract organized crime to our beautiful city." Ms. Wynns responded.

"Your Honor, it was just two thieves."

"Two thieves too many," Ms. Wynns added.

"That's enough. Objection overruled. Continue, Ms. Wynns."

"Here are pictures of a cat and dog on the loose without a leash behind the hotel, terrorizing the other guests." It was a picture of Bread and Butter playing hide and seek and making funny faces at each other in the back of the hotel by the patios.

"And here is a picture of the defendant's attorney, Mr. Counts, watching these dangerous animals run loose on the hotel's grounds. It's so irresponsible."

David asked Stewart, "Did you let them out without a leash?"

"Yes. I mean no. It wasn't like that," Stewart defended himself to David.

"Here is a picture of their Pet Talent Show with someone dressed up in a goldfish costume. Here is a monkey dressed in a suit."

"Now, let me get this straight, Ms. Snipe. At the Pet Talent Show, people dressed up like animals and the animals dressed like people?" Wynns mockingly mused.

"Not everyone," Abby absently blurted out.

The audience laughed.

"Ms. Snipe, what service are we providing to the community based on these pictures?"

"None. Absolutely none. If that hotel doesn't shut down immediately, Savannah won't have any tourists, except for the animals."

"Based on all these disturbing facts, what did the voting citizens of this wonderful community do?"

"We got together and formed our group called the People Against Pets."

"Why?"

"It's not that we don't want people to have pets, as repulsive as they are. It is just that the Pets-By-the-Sea Hotel houses filthy pets in the heart of our tourist district. It's ruining our commercial establishments and hurting business in the area."

"So what action are the People Against Pets petitioning the judge to take?"

"We figured if the court knew about the terrible things going on at the hotel, they'd shut it down immediately," Ms. Snipe concluded.

"And what shall they do with all those pets?" Ms. Wynns asked.

"Those so-called pets belong in a home where they cannot be seen, or locked up in a zoo. If they must be outside, they should be on a farm, far away from the general public. They are a nuisance to society, especially our tourist district."

"Thank you, Ms. Snipe. I couldn't have said it better myself.

The plaintiff rests, Your Honor."

"This doesn't look good," David whispered to Stewart.

"Your turn for cross examination, Mr. Counts."

"No questions, Your Honor."

"No questions?" Debbie whispered back.

"I don't know what else Ms. Snipe has in terms of pictures.

The quicker we get her off the stand the better," Stewart explained.

Meanwhile, on the highway to the courthouse, Gloria told Ralph, "Hurry. We don't want to be late."

"I'm going as fast as I can without getting a ticket."

23

"Mr. Counts, you may begin your direct examination," the judge instructed.

Stewart turned to Debbie and whispered, "Didn't you take some pictures too?"

"I sure did. I happened to have just gotten these developed since we were near the end of the trip." She reached down into her large tote bag. "They're in here somewhere," she said, as she handed them to Mr. Counts to review.

"Mr. Counts, we do not have all day. It's your turn to speak," the judge said with irritation at the delay.

"Yes. Sorry, Your Honor. I am calling Deborah Dents whose pictures tell a very different story."

"Go ahead," the judge said as Debbie took the oath.

"Ms. Dents, did you take these pictures?"

"Yes. I did."

"When did you take them?"

"This week during my stay at the Pets-by-the-Sea Hotel."

"Tell us about them."

"This one is Butter, my pet cat, recovering from the boat ride after Bread, the dog, saved her. It was my fault, not the hotel's, because I didn't follow their instructions to keep Butter's leash fastened to the railing.

When I turned my head, she fell over," she explained.

"What about this picture?"

"This is a picture of the beautiful Pet Care Center. When I came to pick up Butter, I complimented Mike, the pet sitter, on doing such a good job."

"This is Butter and I at the beach party walking along the pier. It was a lot of fun. We met a lot of nice people and their pets. This next one was Butter at the talent show. Doesn't she look cute?"

"I object, Your Honor, we don't want opinions here. Just the facts."

"Objection sustained. She's correct, Ms. Dents. Please stick to the facts," the judge instructed her.

"Do you have any more pictures that you want to show the court?" Stewart asked.

"I have this one of Butter and her friend Bread on the bus tour."

"No further questions of Ms. Dents, Your Honor," Stewart concluded.

"Your cross," the judge instructed Ms. Wynns.

"Don't you know that you endangered the life of an animal when you supposedly forgot to tie her up on the boat ride?"

"Well, yes, but it was an accident." Debbie hung her head.

"Ms. Dents, let me see that picture of the animals on the bus tour. Why are Bread and Butter soaking wet?"

"From the water fountain."

"Tell the court how they ended up in a historic city fountain?"

"We were chasing them all over the place because they got away from us. That's where we stopped them."

"And how did you do that?" Ms. Wynns asked.

"We had to go into the fountain to get them."

"You mean all four of you, a man, a woman, a cat and a dog?"

"Yes, but," Debbie tried to explain further.

"You've answered the question. That's enough for me."

"Any more witnesses, Mr. Counts?" the judge asked.

Debbie was relieved to get off of the witness stand. "How'd I do?"

"Don't ask." Stewart replied.

"Yes, Your Honor. I have one final witness. I call Mr. David Shepherd, the manager and minister of the hotel."

"Mr. Shepherd, tell us how you came to establish the Pets-by-the-Sea Hotel."

"Certainly. I've always had pets in my home. I remember when my mother, who also loved pets, was ill. Our pet cat, Sunshine, used to give her such joy, just being there to comfort her."

"Anything else?"

"When I was raising my son, we used to play wonderful outdoor games with our pet dog, Strength. Taking care of our pets gave my son a sense of responsibility and pride. Our pet pig, Jolly, won first prize at the county fair. With me being a minister and all, I felt that my love for people and pets could be combined to bring them together for a fun-filled vacation, where the owners wouldn't have to leave their dear pets at home every time they wanted to travel.

That's how Pets-by-the-Sea Hotel was established."

"Anything else, Mr. Shepherd?"

"The love we share with our pets often transfers to our love for our fellowman. I've seen couples meet and blossom into a long and loving relationship after staying at our hotel."

"How sappily romantic," Ms. Wynns yawned in a whisper to her client.

"There's the courthouse," Gloria shouted to Ralph.

Ralph pulled the station wagon into a parking space. In their rush, they forgot about Bread and Butter in the back seat. They closed and locked the door to the station wagon with Bread and Butter still inside on a hot summer day.

Ralph and Gloria ran up the stairs to the lobby.

"Where is the courtroom?" Gloria asked the information clerk.

"Which one? We have several," the clerk replied.

"The one where the wedding is taking place," Ralph said.

"Which one? We have several."

"Never mind. Ralph you go that way and I'll go this way."

Gloria pointed in opposite directions to cover the courtrooms.

"I don't believe I'm doing this," Ralph mumbled, rushing down the hall and peeking into courtrooms. Ralph poked his head in a courtroom and saw the back of a couple taking their wedding vows.

He shouted, "Stop the wedding!"

The couple turned around and Ralph quickly realized it was not Stewart and Debbie.

"Sorry. Wrong wedding." He slowly closed the door.

"Who was that man?" The groom asked his bride.

"I have no idea." She shrugged her shoulders. They turned back around to complete the wedding ceremony and noticed that the judge had a strange smirk on his face.

The judge said without missing a beat, "Shall we proceed?"

At another courtroom, Gloria saw a wedding taking place through the small window. She swung open the door and busted down the aisle. "Don't do it!" she shouted. This couple turned around. It was not Stewart and Debbie.

"Excuse me. Carry on," Gloria said as she backed out, almost bumping into the door behind her.

"Who was that?" asked the bride.

"I don't remember. I mean, nobody," the groom said with a total look of puzzlement on his face. The bride stood there for a minute.

"We get these interruptions all the time. Shall we continue?" the judge lightheartedly said.

Back in the station wagon, there was no one in sight. It was mid-morning and most people were already at work or in the courthouse in hearings. Bread and Butter were panting from being overheated.

All of a sudden, the station wagon's alarm went off. The horns blew. The lights flashed and a loud speaker bellowed, "Pet inside! Please remove pet inside!" The hotel station wagon was equipped with an internal motion detector that was set to go off after three minutes. If a pet was accidentally left inside, the motion detector picked up the movement and triggered the alarm.

It was blaring even louder, "Pet inside! Please remove pet inside!" The doors automatically unlocked and the windows automatically rolled down.

Bread helped to shove Butter out of the station wagon's window first. Bread immediately jumped out the window after Butter. They ran up the courthouse steps.

"Halt! Where are you going?" the security guard shouted as Butter and Bread ran right past him.

The guard ran right behind them. Butter and Bread dashed up the stairs.

Bread sniffed for Stewart's scent as they ran. They dashed up another flight of stairs.

"Stop or I'll shoot," the guard warned.

"Shoot who? You're not going to shoot that poor cat and dog. They might be someone's pets." The information clerk, who had up until this time been docile, saw the pets running up the stairs and the guard in hot pursuit.

"Get out of my way," the guard said to the clerk, putting the gun back into his holster. He continued to run up the stairs.

"Call the dog catcher, now!" the guard ordered the clerk.

"You call 'em," said the clerk as she turned away to go back to her desk. She had photos of her own pets plastered all over her workstation. She sat back down, looked and smiled at the photos of her pet cat and dog. She looked over on her counter and smiled at her pet bird in a cage.

"This is the third floor and fifth wedding we've crashed.

We haven't found them yet," a tired, out-of-breath Ralph said.

"Keep looking. There's just one more floor left," the equally out-of-breath Gloria said. "Let's take the elevator this time." Ralph pushed the up button.

Which button to we push?" asked Ralph.

"Put any one higher up." Gloria was just as puzzled.

"This elevator is so slow. We could have walked up the final flight by now," Gloria complained.

"Are you finished?" the judge asked Stewart.

"Wait. May I say one final thing, Your Honor?"

"You've had your chance, but if you'll be brief go ahead. We have other items on the agenda today."

Debbie whispered to Stewart, "What are you going to say?"

Stewart whispered back, "I have no idea."

"Your Honor, we just ask that when you decide," Stewart stammered.

Just at that moment Bread and Butter dashed down the aisle to Stewart and Debbie. Instinctively Stewart reached his arms out to hug Bread.

"Bread? What are you doing here?" he hugged Bread like he hadn't seen him in years.

Right behind Bread was Butter, who ran straight to Debbie. "Butter. Oh Butter!" Debbie said as she reached her arms out to Butter for a hug.

The judge yelled, "Who let the dog and cat in?

Restrain them immediately!"

Stewart hastily continued, "As I was saying, these are our pets. We love them. They have brought great joy to our lives.

Is closing the door on one of the few things we can do for them, any way you want to treat man's best friends? See how loving they are?"

Just then, Bread did a trick that Stewart had taught him to do at the Talent Show by standing up on his hind feet and turning around in a circle. Everyone in the room laughed, except for Ms. Wynns and Ms. Snipe. Bread spun around like a top. The citizens laughed some more. Butter did a trick too, by rolling a cup around on the floor. The citizens continued laughing, even the judge. Bread went up to one friendly citizen that smiled and started wagging his tail. The citizen patted him on the head and Bread waved his whole body.

"Isn't he cute! Can I pat him?" said an old lady in the audience.

Bread went over to her for a pat. Butter instinctively found a cat friendly citizen that reached out to pet her. Butter purred with each pat.

"Aren't they darling?" another citizen commented.

"What cute names, 'Bread and Butter,'" one citizen said.

Bread and Butter started playing with each other and having a good time.

"Look. They get along so well," another citizen said.

Ms. Snipe whispered in Ms. Wynns' ear, "We should have brought the pigs in to show how pets really act."

"Too risky," Wynns explained to Ms. Snipe.

Even the merchants were warming up to them.

"Me next," another citizen said.

"Quiet! Order in the court!" the judge shouted. "Proceed with your closing statement."

Ms. Wynns closed with, "See for yourself, the mayhem pets create. Close the hotel, now!"

"Your Honor," Stewart concluded, "I rest my case in your wise judgment, to keep the pets with the people!"

"I'm ready to make my ruling from the bench. In order for there to be a nuisance under common law, 'the gravity of the harm must outweigh the utility of the actor's conduct.' While the 'gravity of the harm' is the sight of pets in a tourist district which may be offensive to some tourists or business owners, the 'utility of the conduct,' or put another way, the 'social value of the conduct,' is the joy and happiness that sweet and charming pets give to their owners and the public, is much greater in this case," the judge opined.

"What does that mean?" David asked Stewart.

Judge Wright continued, "Therefore, it is the decision of the court that Pets-by-the-Sea Hotel is not a nuisance.

Therefore, the People Against Pets' petition to enjoin the hotel's operations is denied. Case dismissed!" He pounded his gavel to formally end the hearing.

"We won, we won!" David shouted with joy. Almost every one started jumping up and down in jubilation. Bread went up to the grumpy photographer from People Against Pets, wagging his tail and licking her face. "You are a charming pet." Ms. Snipe's frown melted into a smile.

Lena Wynns packed up her briefcase. Bread and Butter walked up to her. Bread and Butter both extended their paws as a gesture of peace. Wynns reached down and hugged them both. She said with a smile and whisper in their ears, "I don't want to see you two in court again. It's bad for my reputation."

In all the commotion and excitement, no one noticed that Gloria and Ralph had just entered the courtroom.

"I object!" Ralph shouted.

The people and judge stopped to turn around to look at them.

"To what?" the judge asked.

"To the marriage," Gloria shouted, still out of breath.

"What marriage? There's no marriage being performed in here," the judge replied.

"There isn't?" a surprised Ralph said.

Gloria stood with her hair all over her head, mismatched shoes and t-shirt half on, not to mention the hit and miss powder puff. Ralph hadn't done much better, having grabbed yesterday's wrinkled shirt and having forgotten to put on his belt. In his rush up the courthouse stairs, his pants started falling down. There he stood with his orange and brown giraffe design, boxer shorts from U-Save, exposed. Here they were, frozen at the folly of their flippant plans to foil a marriage that never took place.

"Uh oh," Ralph meekly uttered, looking at all the people, but speaking to Gloria in a low still voice. "It looks like there is no marriage," he repeated to her.

She said to Ralph, through a forced smile and unmoving teeth, "Now what do we do?"

"Gloria?" Stewart approached her in disbelief and shock.

"Ralph?" Debbie said at the sight of Ralph. "What are you doing here? I get it. You brought Bread and Butter to us.

Thanks. We appreciate that." Debbie graciously smiled. David came over and touched Ralph on his shoulder, as he whispered, "Your giraffe's showing."

Ralph looked down at his half fallen pants. He almost choked as he grabbed his pants to keep them from falling completely to the ground. He started slowly backing out of the courtroom.

"Happy to help out." Ralph waved good-bye with his one free hand.

"What perfect timing. Thanks," Stewart said to Gloria. "You're welcome. Anything for a friend."

Abby approached Gloria with raised eyebrows and whispered in her ear, "Did you have a rough night, dear?"

Gloria looked down at her shoes and saw a mismatched pair on her feet.

Just before exiting the room entirely, Ralph said, "We've got to go."

"Got to go. Here are your pets. Bye," Gloria repeated as she made a quick turnaround. She grabbed Ralph by the arm to make a fast retreat out of the courthouse.

"See you back at the hotel," Debbie waved at Ralph and Gloria.

David turned to Stewart and shook his hand. "I knew we would win. I just knew it in my heart," he said.

"I'm glad you knew that, because I had my doubts for awhile," Stewart modestly acknowledged.

Lena Wynns walked over to Stewart and shook his hand.

"What can I say? I'm no match against Bread and Butter," she said with a laugh.

The People Against Pets members even warmed up to Bread and Butter who continued to make the rounds like celebrities.

"We have our closing Fashion and Awards Banquet tonight.

Plus we have something to celebrate. Are you coming?"" Abby asked Stewart and Debbie.

"We'll be there," Stewart beamed.

"Yes, we will," Debbie said while looking at Stewart and smiling.

"Will you join me at my table?" Stewart's eyes locked on Debbie.

"I wouldn't miss it for the world," Debbie replied with eyes locked on Stewart.

"Let's roll. We've got a banquet to get ready for," David beamed from the exhilarating victory.

24

Stewart with Bread, Debbie with Butter, David and Abby left the courthouse in the hotel car.

Stewart paused and asked Debbie, "I didn't know you knew Ralph."

"I didn't know you knew Ralph either," Debbie questioned too.

"I just met him this week. When did you meet him?" he probed.

"I've known him for years. He lives in my apartment building."

"He does? Why was he down here?"

"He said he had a gig but I believe he followed me down here. He's been trying to get me to date him but I've refused."

"How serious is this?" a concerned Stewart asked.

"Don't get excited, Stewart. We only had a few encounters Nothing happened. He just can't seem to take 'no' for an answer."

"I'll teach him how to take 'no,'" an irritated and protective Stewart said.

"Don't worry about him. He is harmless. Besides, he hasn't stopped us from enjoying each other." She tried to change the subject.

"I'm not so sure of that. Ralph is the guy that's been

coaching me on how to get chicks, I means girls, I mean a lady, you," he said stumbling over his own words.

"What! I can't believe you listened to someone as inexperienced as Ralph. He wouldn't know what to do with a woman if she threw herself at him."

"What? How do you know so much about Ralph?"

"Like I said. We're in the same apartment building and some of the other ladies have been trying to get him to go to bed with them but he's always been afraid to do it, you know. Excuse us David and Abby. Just pretend you aren't hearing this conversation."

"What were you saying?" David joked.

"He's a virgin, plain and simple. He knows he is safe with me, because I have a tendency to pulverize anybody that comes near me."

"I get that part. I get it now. Ralph kept telling me to do the things to you that would tick you off so that I would come out on the losing end with you. Why that low down..."

David interrupted the conversation, "Stewart, remember our Bible lesson this week, when we talked about forgiveness?

Just pause and think for a moment. Who is the successful guy that is with Debbie right now?"

Stewart thought for a moment. "You're right. It's me," Stewart smiled at Debbie who smiled back.

As the car traveled down the road a few more miles a revelation dawned on Debbie.

"I noticed you called Gloria by her name. Do you know her?" she asked.

"Gloria? She's my secretary," he nonchalantly

replied.

"What? You brought your secretary down here? I sensed you were a hard worker, but isn't that a bit much?" she said with concern.

"It's not like that. She didn't come down here to work."

"You mean you've been seeing me and your secretary at the same time?" Debbie's anger swelled. "David, stop the car. I'm getting out of here. Don't try to stop me, or else you'll be lying on the car floor doubled over from a cracked rib," she yelled at Stewart.

"It's not what you think. Let me explain," he said in desperation.

"Weren't you two paying attention in Bible Class last Wednesday? Can't we all just get along and behave properly?" David reminded them.

"If only people would take the time to listen to each other, a lot of their fears and conflicts would go away," David continued.

Abby, quiet up to this moment, spoke, "Now daughter, didn't you tell us you have a ministry called SafeCity, to promote non-violence? Why don't you at least listen to what Stewart has to say?"

"What is there to listen to? He has a girlfriend, his secretary of all people, at the same time that he is talking to me. Case closed. When did you have time to date her when you were with me so much?" she cross-examined him.

"I didn't date her. She came here on her own, without telling me."

"A likely story. You can do better than that," Debbie huffed with arms crossed.

"Ralph came down here to see you without telling you, didn't he?" Stewart reminded her.

"Yes, but that was different."

"Why didn't you tell me your lover-boy was here, huh? You've got something to hide?"

"No. Because he doesn't mean anything to me."

"Neither does Gloria. I work with her and she's a good secretary, but that's all. She's been trying to get me to notice her but I have never been interested in her. That's the truth."

Silence. Now Abby continued, "See, you both have others who care about you, maybe just a bit over zealous. What's most important is that you care about each other. Isn't that what counts?"

More silence.

"I guess you're right. Maybe I did jump to conclusions," Debbie said, now calmed down. "Now that I think about this week, Gloria must have befriended me so that she could break us up," Debbie thought out loud.

"What do you mean, befriended you?"

"She told me that men like flashy dressers who are demanding of their resources."

"She told you that?" he said with a laugh.

"What's so funny?"

"Gloria is a very nice person, even though she is not my type. She is a little naïve when it comes to men. I really don't think you should be getting advice about men from her, of all people."

"But she told me she could get any man she wanted."

"Not if you count her batting average at work, which

I'd say is 'zero.'"

"Zero? What do you mean?"

"Guys have taken her out on one date and come back to the office saying 'never again.'"

"What happened?"

"All I know, since I've never dated her, is that she tells me when the guys start to come on to her, she looks surprised and starts reading the Bible to them, the part about 'Thou shalt not commit fornication.'"

"What's wrong with that?"

"When you dress like a flower, flaunting your nectar, you attract hungry bees who want a little taste."

"Oh. I get the picture."

"You're not listening, are you David and Abby?" Stewart checked.

"What did you say?" David smiled. "Here we are safe and sound, back at the hotel. You young kids, get some rest before tonight's Awards Banquet."

"We'll send you any kind of food you want for room service, no extra charge," Abby added.

"Thanks. Can I have some more gourmet dog biscuits?" Stewart asked for Bread.

Bread waved his tail.

"The biscuits are on their way, " Abby laughed.

"The Pet Salon is open this afternoon, if you want to spruce up Bread and Butter before dinner. Tell them to put any grooming service you want for Bread and Butter on the house," David extended to them.

Everyone, including Bread and Butter, piled out of the car.

"I'll have Butter at the salon in a few hours. She could use a bath," Debbie said.

"I'll take Bread to the salon also," Stewart said.

"Great. I'll tell the groomers to expect you. See you all tonight."

Abby and David remained in the lobby for a moment. "Are you thinking what I'm thinking?" Abby asked David.

"What? Food?" David guessed.

"We'll get to that, but maybe we should make a call to Gloria and Ralph, just to see if they need anything to wear for this evening," Abby suggested.

"Good idea. I'll give Ralph a call and you can call Gloria."

"Good thought, dear. I know just the thing for her."

Back at the hotel, "You really blew that one," Ralph said to Gloria on the telephone in his room.

"Me? You were the one that drove to the courthouse. If it was such a dumb idea, why didn't you stop me?"

"Because, I didn't want to see you embarrass yourself. But no, you wouldn't listen to me."

"Now we've both embarrassed each other," she said with disgust.

"Speak for yourself, doll."

"What? Look, this team effort thing is not working out so well. I think I'm better off on my own."

"That suits me just fine. By the way, put on matching shoes the next time you go out on your own, kid."

"You've got a lot of nerve, with your pants falling

down, although I must admit the giraffe shorts were kind of cute," she laughed.

"That bra strap showing on one shoulder, that was really interesting. Is that the new thing now?" Ralph snickered.

"We did look kind of funny standing in front of all of those people."

"That's putting it mildly, sweetheart," Ralph added with amusement.

"Look, thanks Ralph. I've gotten you in enough hot water this week. I'm all out of ideas. I should be more considerate of your feelings."

"We've just got this last night in Savannah, to pull this thing together," he said with a tone of seriousness.

"I know. We are running out of time before we head back to Detroit tomorrow," Gloria added with a tone of sadness in her voice.

"I've got an idea."

"I'm in shock. You do?"

"Why don't we pretend to be out on a date and make them jealous? When they see that we are pretending to enjoy each other, they will come around to our way of thinking. What do you think of that?"

"You mean we are going to pretend to like each other? I don't know. That will be pretty difficult," she teased.

"Come on, I'm serious."

"Okay."

"I'll do this only under one condition," he conditioned the arrangement while returning to his lighter side.

"What's that?"

"That you don't get carried away with all this pretending thing, and try to seduce me," Ralph joked.

"You're safe with me."

25

Gloria's phone rang. "Hello?" Gloria answered.

"Hi. It's Abby. I was wondering if you've selected your outfit for this evening? I know a great store that might have something nice for you."

"I do have a sequined mini dress."

"That sounds nice dear, however, you may want to look at a few floor lengths for comparison."

"Why not? I like to shop."

Abby took Gloria to get a whole new outfit from top to bottom. She also took Gloria to her salon and shared her favorite perfume, 'Simply Pure.' While they were shopping, Abby gave Gloria a few pointers on how to act like a refined lady at the night's formal affair.

Soon after Abby called Gloria, David called Ralph.

"Hello."

"Hi Ralph, this is David. Got a few minutes to come to my office?"

"Sure, what's up?"

"I may have some extra tuxedos that you can wear tonight, unless you've brought your own?"

"I didn't have time to pack everything. I would like to see them. Got any shoes while you're at it? Tennis shoes and tuxes don't go together too well, so I've been told."

"As a matter of fact, I can call a shoe store and have them deliver your size."

"Great. I'm on my way."

While trying on the tuxedo and picking out matching accessories, David gave Ralph a few pointers on being a gentleman, the kind that attracts women, not repels them.

"Learn these Bible scriptures before tonight and you will undoubtedly make a great impression," he coached Ralph. "My personal barber will give you a great hairstyle. He's across the street and can see you this afternoon."

"Sounds good to me, David. This is what I call hospitality."

The Pet Salon this Friday afternoon was very busy with shampoos and haircuts.

"I heard that Stewart saved the hotel with the help of his pet dog, Bread, along with Butter, Debbie's pet," Grace, the teenaged groomer, said.

"Me too, child. Isn't that wonderful?" Faith, another teenaged groomer said.

"Look who just walked in the door," Hope said, the third groomer in her early twenties. "Welcome to our Pet Salon, Debbie. What can we do for Butter today?" she asked.

"Hi. I'd like for you to give her a bath, clip her nails and brush her fur, so that she will look real pretty tonight."

"We'll be happy to give her the deluxe treatment. After all, she is very special to us here at the hotel," Hope said.

"Thanks."

"We'll call you up when she's ready and return her to your room," Charity, the fourth groomer, a teenager, said.

"Great. Butter, be sweet," Debbie said as she hugged Butter before returning to her room to get ready for the evening.

The groomers continued their chatter.

"Debbie and Stewart are the talk of the hotel," Faith said.

"No?" Hope said in disbelief.

"Yes. They've been a hot number this week," Charity said.

"They are a cute couple," Grace said.

"You know that they have been going to bed with each other every night," Faith said.

"No." Hope said.

"Yes. You know you can't keep a good looking man like Stewart and not be going to bed with him. She's got to give something up, if you know what I mean," Hope said.

"You're right about that," Charity agreed.

"Not necessarily. Debbie and Stewart just might like each other's company. They worked real well together on that trial. There is more to a good relationship than the physical. I think they have a spiritual bond," Grace observed.

"Child, have you been in church too long? You need to get out more, into the real world," Faith said.

"Give me something I can touch and feel," Hope laughed. The groomers laughed.

"Let's start with that bath, Ms. Butter," Hope picked

217

Butter up to take her to the bath area.

Butter saw the water and squirmed to get away.

"We have a special shampoo for you," Hope sung with a smile, dipping Butter into the tub and lathering her up.

At about this time, Stewart brought Bread into the Pet Salon.

"Stewart, is this the famous Bread we've heard so much about?" Faith greeted them upon seeing Stewart arrive with Bread in tow.

"He is Bread. I didn't know he was famous."

"What can we do for our hero today?" Faith asked.

"I want a complete general grooming job, the works. David said everything was free."

"We will give him the extra special care package. We'll bring him to your room as soon as he's fixed up," Faith smiled as Stewart handed Bread over to her.

"Great. See you in a few," Stewart said as he patted Bread on the head and left.

Bread very reluctantly went with Faith to the bath area.

"But what about that Ralph guy? He likes Debbie too," Hope continued after Stewart walked out of the salon.

Hope massaged Butter's head with the shampoo.

"Debbie doesn't give him any hope. He needs to move on and check me out. I think he's handsome in a rugged way," Faith said.

"A man like that is always chasing after what he can't get," Charity concluded.

"I think that's just because Debbie is not the right woman for him. When the right one comes along, he won't have such a hard time," Grace surmised.

"Child, where do you get your thoughts from? Any woman can get any man as long as she uses the right tricks on him," Hope said.

Hope started lathering up Butter's belly side.

"Doesn't that feel good? Yes?" Hope asked and answered her own question.

"How are we doing there, Bread? What a handsome dog you are. After the bath we are going to make you look even better," Faith smiled as she took Bread to the bath area.

"Okay, let's rinse you off with our fur conditioner," Hope said.

"Gloria, poor thing, doesn't have Ralph or Stewart," Faith said.

"And she never will, because she's too loose. I can tell by the way she dresses and throws herself at men," Charity said.

"You can't always go by how a person dresses. You have to know their heart. She might be a highly-principled person," Grace said.

"Get real. This is the twenty-first century. Who's following any morals these days?" Hope said.

"It's all about getting what you can now, because you never know what you won't get later," Charity commented.

"That's not what I've been taught from the Bible," Grace said.

"I don't want to hear about that Bible stuff right

now. I want to know who is Debbie going to sleep with next?" Faith said.

"Somebody's been buying those designer clothes she's been wearing," Charity laughed.

"You got that right," Hope laughed.

"These nails are too long," Hope said. Clip, clip, clip went the clippers on Butter's toenails.

"Gloria, the Glitter Girl, is another story. I hope she hurries and finds a man who can tame that wardrobe," Faith laughed.

"I wonder what she's going to wear tonight?" Charity mused.

"Whatever it is, you'll have to wear sunglasses to shield you from the brightness," Hope laughed.

"Wasn't that a nice bath, Bread? Let's dry you off," Faith said after giving Bread a bath.

"I know who does want a part of her," Faith said.

"Who, girl?" Charity inquired.

"That Ralph guy, with the parakeet," Faith surmised.

"How do you know that, pray tell?" Charity asked.

"They are always fighting. They call that the mating dance," Faith said.

"Mating what? Have you been looking at too many educational TV specials?" Hope said.

"It's true. Some of the same behaviors that lower animals practice to get their mates, us humans do too," Faith informed them.

"Girl, you've been in school too long," Hope said.

"It's time to get your nails clipped, Bread. Hand me your paw," Faith said. Bread handed his paw over to her. "That's a nice dog," she smiled.

"I can tell you from my street experience that Ralph likes her all right, but it's not because of a mating dance. Look at the way she is dressing. A guy would have to be blind not to be just a little interested in something," Charity said.

"It's more than that between Ralph and Gloria," Grace said.

"How do you mean?" Charity asked.

"They seem to have a lot in common. They like to go out and be around people. They are both high-energy people and they both have flashy styles. They talk a lot to each other. I think that if they ever stopped running after folks that don't want them, they just might discover each other," Grace said.

"Child, stay out of them books. The way they fight and fuss? No way," Hope said.

"I'm with you sister," Charity said.

"Me too," Faith said.

"Bread, are we ready for a nice brushing?" Faith asked.

"You're going to look so neat tonight," Faith smiled.

"I can hardly wait to see what Miss Gloria is going to wear tonight. If there were a Glitter Girl award, she'd win it," Hope said as she brushed Butter's hair.

"And for the worst dressed, Stewart would win that," Charity laughed.

"Don't forget 'worst tipper' for him also," Faith laughed.

"What about Ralph? He ought to get an award for the Best Pest," Hope laughed.

"While we are at it, how about Miss Debbie?" Charity asked.

"What about the Karate Queen?" Faith said, as the groomers laughed.

"Butter, you are going to look so pretty tonight with this pink ribbon on your head," Hope said.

"We should not be talking about our guests like that. It's not Christian-like," Grace warned her co-workers.

"Okay, let's talk about our bosses," Faith laughed.

"Child, did you hear about Ms. Martha. I heard she killed a mouse, single-footedly," Hope laughed.

"That news was all over the hotel. People are calling her Martha, the Mouse Terminator," Charity laughed.

"Ms. Martha is so good at killing mice, she should open up her own business and put on her business card, 'Got Mice? Get Martha,'" Faith laughed.

"I think she should register her feet as a dangerous weapon," Hope laughed.

"Let's hope Abby doesn't find out. She prides herself on running a dignified and proper establishment," Grace told them.

"Speaking of Abby, they should call her Fast Abby," Faith said.

"Why do you say that?" Hope asked.

"David didn't have a chance when she first met him. The story goes, from the first moment she laid eyes on him, she fed him and adored every inch of him," Charity said.

"And what's wrong with that?" Grace asked.

"You shouldn't be too nice to a man. It spoils him," Faith explained.

"That's a thought," Hope agreed.

"Spoil me first," Charity laughed.

Bread was getting a nice brisk fur brushing.

Bread wagged his tail in total enjoyment.

"You'd better be careful talking about the owners. What if David walked in and heard you? We'd all be in trouble," Grace warned.

"Ole Shep? We'll talk about him too," Faith laughed.

"Let me tell you about Ole Shep. Did you know that he..." Faith started to say.

Just at that moment, the door to the salon opened and David unexpectedly walked in.

"Good afternoon groomers. Are we taking good care of our pets today?" David cheerfully asked.

"Yes, Mr. Shepherd," the groomers said in unison.

26

It was Friday, the night of the hotel's Awards Banquet, when pets and their owners got to wear their most elegant outfits.

"You look freshened up," Stewart said as he stood to hold the chair for Debbie to sit down at the table. Debbie was wearing a crisp white organza silk see-through ¾ length jacket with a matching scoop neck sleeveless silk blouse and matching silk straight-line floor length skirt. She also wore white satin pumps and a matching small white satin purse. Her perfume was "Cool Breeze."

Butter was by her side, on a leash.

"Hi Butter, what a pretty pink ribbon on your head," Abby noticed.

"Thank you. The salon put that ribbon on Butter. I think it's kind of cute too," Debbie said.

"Before you sit down, I want to take a picture of you and Butter," Stewart said as he pulled out a disposable no-name brand camera from his suit pocket. "Smile for the camera," Stewart said as Debbie and Butter stood up straight and smiled.

Snap. "Thanks. Those should come out really nice. Wait, before you sit down, Debbie. I'd like to take a picture of you by yourself. Wait a few more minutes, as I turn to the next exposure."

He pushed the lever to advance the film forward. "Hold it, while I wait for the red light to come on. Okay, hold it. There we go."

Snap. "I want to save the rest for the Awards program. These cameras aren't cheap you know."

"Hi Bread. Don't you look spiffy tonight? I hope you get an Award tonight. You certainly deserve one. You too Butter," David said with a wink.

"You think so?" Debbie asked Stewart.

"I wonder if there are any monetary gifts with those Awards?" Stewart asked.

David moved on to the next table without hearing that last comment.

Debbie scanned through the printed program, "There's no mention of that, but I'm sure the trophies will be very nice."

Meanwhile, Ralph arrived at Gloria's door to escort her to the Banquet. She opened the door.

"Wow, Gloria, You look gorgeous," Ralph said as he looked at her long flowing peach organza evening gown, with matching peach high heel slippers and dainty pearl earrings.

She did not have a stitch of gold anywhere.

"You don't look so bad yourself in that black tux."

"You like it, really?"

"Yes. It makes you look so distinguished."

"I like the way you painted and decorated the goldfish bowl with green leaves and ribbons, Gloria dear."

"Thanks."

"The parakeet cage on wheels. That's pretty original."

"Thanks for the compliment, gorgeous."

"Shall we?" Ralph extended his arm for Gloria to take, like a gentleman.

"Remember, Ralph, we've got to put on a good act, or they will be on to us."

"You can count on me, doll," Ralph said as they made their way through the entrance of the ballroom.

"There they are. Let's sit at their table," Gloria pointed in their direction.

"My pleasure," Ralph obliged as he walked lightly on his feet.

"May we join you?" Ralph asked with Gloria still on his arm.

Stewart looked up in amazement at the two of them together.

"I'm not sure," Stewart began to say.

"Good evening my children. Welcome to the Banquet," David, who was wearing a black tuxedo, greeted Ralph and Gloria.

"What two lovely couples," Abby by his side, added. She wore a stunning strapless black taffeta, bodice fitting, full skirt floor length evening gown.

Debbie nudged Stewart at his coattail as if to say, "Be nice."

"Sure. Have a seat," Stewart reluctantly said.

"Folks. Enjoy the program," David said with a smile. He and Abby walked away to greet the other guests.

Ralph held the chair for Gloria to sit down.

"Thank you, sweetheart," she graciously acknowledged Ralph's chivalry.

"My joy. My dumpling. May I get you something to drink, dear?" Ralph politely asked of Gloria.

"Yes, please, darling," Gloria replied with a bashful smile and nod, eyes never leaving Ralph.

Ralph got up to get Gloria something at the cash juice bar.

"I'm a little thirsty myself, Stewart," Debbie said to Stewart.

"I believe the beverage comes with the dinner. Can you wait? Here, try some water. It's very good." Stewart reached for the water pitcher.

Trying not to be disagreeable, Debbie replied, "Of course."

"Here you are, sugums," Ralph said as he handed Gloria her juice.

"You look nice, Debbie," Ralph said. Before she could say "thank you," he turned to Gloria and said, "You look ravishing in that color. You are a true Georgia peach, doll."

"Don't overdo it," Gloria whispered in his ear with a giggle.

"Thank you, snookums," she said.

"We've got to make them believe this, remember?" Ralph whispered back as he touched her ear ever so gently. He put his arms around her.

At first, Gloria was caught off guard. She relaxed and leaned into him.

Stewart and Debbie were just sitting there staring at the two lovebirds.

"Excuse our manners," Gloria said with a blush. "Have you enjoyed your week here?"

"Yes. It's been great," Debbie began to say.

"Darling. Not now." Ralph distracted Gloria with his under-the-table excursion of his hand on her thigh. She promptly pinched him, causing a quick withdrawal.

"I wonder what's for dinner?" Stewart changed the subject.

"I'm sure it will be nice, whatever it is," Debbie said.

Ralph returned to his memorized lines, "Oh my dove, that art in the clefts of the rock, in the secret places of the stairs, let me see thy countenance, let me hear thy voice; for sweet is thy voice, and thy countenance is comely. Turn away thine eyes from me, for they have overcome me, O prince's daughter! The joints of thy thighs are like jewels, the work of the hands of a cunning workman."

Gloria was speechless.

"Is that Shakespeare?" Debbie curiously asked.

"No. It's from a Song that Solomon wrote." Ralph's eyes still affixed on Gloria.

Gloria obliged by allowing him to hold her hand, as she blushed.

"How nice," Debbie commented.

"Sounds corny to me," Stewart complained.

"Welcome to our Fashion Show and Awards Banquet Dinner," David announced. "We have some wonderful models, our pets, modeling the latest fashions in pet couture. So sit back, relax, and enjoy the food. The master of ceremonies tonight is my son, Timothy."

"Thank you, Dad, for that long introduction of me. Next time, don't tell them my life history," Timothy laughed with his hyena laugh.

"We will now have my dad back again to bless the food, although some of our guests have started chomping on the dog biscuits already." Timothy looked over to where Bread was sitting.

"Let us bow our heads in prayer," David began.

"Try to keep the oinking down," Timothy mumbled at a table of pigs.

"Dear Heavenly Father, we praise Your mighty and matchless name. We thank You for all of Your creations, from the littlest critters to the largest beasts. We humbly ask You to bless this special occasion. May every pet and person here tonight find peace, joy and happiness in obedience to Your will."

"When is he going to end?" Stewart whispered to Debbie.

"I'm getting hungry."

"Shush," she whispered back to him.

"Finally, dear Lord, in the name of Jesus Christ, our Savior, bless this food, the people who prepared it and the pets and folks who will eat it for the nourishment of their bodies. Feed them dear Lord, not only food for the body but also spiritual wisdom and guidance for their soul. Amen."

"Amen," Stewart eagerly said with fork already in hand.

"Honey bunch, want some fruit?" Gloria asked Ralph, as she lifted a grape to Ralph's lips for him to eat from her hand.

She moved up his thigh with her other hand, as payback for his earlier antics. Ralph grabbed her wandering hand and squeezed it, until she retreated.

"Don't go there," he whispered in her ear.

After a nibble or two of the grapes, Ralph reached for the shrimp and dipped it in the shrimp cocktail before raising it up to Gloria's lips. Somehow, as she took a nibble, it accidentally slipped out of his hand and fell down into her cleavage.

"I'm so sorry lambkin," Ralph said in a sincere apology.

He was about to retrieve it when Gloria stood up, gritted her teeth with a smile and said under her breath, "Don't even think about it." Openly, Gloria said, "Excuse me, while I use the ladies room."

"I see you and Gloria are hitting it off real well," Debbie noted.

"Yes. It was just one of those things. It hit me like a bolt of lightning," Ralph smiled.

Debbie mumbled, "probably from all those blows to your head."

Stewart frowned at her insensitive remark.

"I'm just a little curious. How did you and Gloria meet?" Stewart asked.

"It seems like I've known her all my life, but actually we met when we checked into the hotel together, I mean, at the same time. No. I would never disrespect a sweet lady like Gloria by trying to stay in the same room. I'm too much of a gentleman to do that," Ralph brushed off his lapel in a smug kind of way.

"You could have fooled me," mumbled Debbie. Stewart gave her another stern look.

"Excuse me, I've got to go to the ladies room," she said. In the ladies room, Debbie happened to see Gloria drying her dress with a hair blow dryer.

"I see you and Ralph kind of like each other?" Debbie

probed.

"'Like' isn't the word for it. He's every woman's dream. I couldn't ask for a more charming and polite gentleman."

"Are we talking about the same Ralph?" a surprised Debbie asked.

"All I know is that I don't know how you ever let him go, but thanks. Your loss is my gain. This dress is as dry as it's going to get. I've got to get back to Ralph. He misses me so much when I'm gone too long."

Just before Gloria exited the ladies room, "Have you ever seen a more handsome man in tux?"

Debbie also returned to her table from the ladies room. As she walked back to their table, she noticed that all the male guests in the room were wearing tuxedos except Stewart.

"Maybe the hotel forgot to tell him," she thought.

Debbie stood at her table waiting for Stewart to assist her by holding the chair for her to sit down. Stewart was busy eating the appetizers.

He finally looked up. "Excuse me, I didn't see you standing there. The food's good." Debbie began to simmer as he eventually pulled the chair out for her. Debbie motioned Girard, the waiter, over to her once she saw that the entrée was steaks.

"Is there something you want?"

"Yes, Girard. May I have a vegetarian plate please?"

"Certainly. I'll get one for you as soon as I place these dinners down."

Ralph and Gloria noticed that Debbie didn't have her dinner plate. They decided to wait for her plate to come.

Stewart started eating without noticing that no one else was eating.

"Could you pass the salt and pepper shaker?" Stewart asked.

Debbie stared at him with a strange look.

"Please?" he corrected himself.

Debbie, sensing it was a lost cause, reached out to hand the shakers to him. That's when he noticed that no one else was eating. He hesitated and then said, "Thanks." He proceeded to salt and pepper his entrée, but feeling all eyes on him, he put his fork down to wait with the others.

"Sure hope it doesn't get cold," Stewart mumbled looking at his food.

"Here you are, Miss," Girard said as he placed her dinner in front of her.

"Thanks," Debbie said with a smile on her face, but disgust in her heart over Stewart's lack of tact.

"Let's eat," Ralph chimed.

Stewart noticed that Debbie was eating various colorful vegetables on her plate except for her grilled mushrooms.

"Are you going to eat those mushrooms? They'll go good with my steak," he asked her, with eyes focused on her mushrooms.

Before Debbie could respond, Stewart reached over with his fork and stabbed her mushrooms with his fork, returning them, like caught prey, to his plate.

Debbie's face got real tense, but Stewart was too busy enjoying his meal to notice.

"Are you enjoying your food, buttercup?" Ralph

asked Gloria.

"It is truly divine, dear. Everything tastes better with you here to enjoy it with me," Gloria swooned.

"How about you, honey?" Gloria asked Ralph.

"It's delectable, exquisite and so very good, gorgeous, but not as good as the sight of you," he smiled.

"Ralph, you say the most charming things."

"What kind of dessert would you like?" Girard asked, showing an assortment of gourmet pies and cakes displayed on the brass and glass butler cart.

"No thank you," Gloria said. "I'm watching my figure."

"No dessert for me, thank you. I've got my sugar pie already," Ralph said gazing into Gloria's eyes.

"None for me, thank you," Debbie said.

"I'll take hers," Stewart interjected, "I never want to turn down good gourmet and free food."

Debbie was feeling unsettled and perturbed by Stewart's behavior.

"May I have this dance with you, princess?" Ralph asked, while extending his hand of invitation to Gloria.

"You certainly may," Gloria giggled as she joined her hand to his. They went onto the floor to a fast playing song. Ralph twirled her around, keeping up with every beat of the music and their steps. "How are we doing?" Gloria asked. With another twirl, Ralph flung her away from his body and back again into his arms.

"I think it's working. They seem to be watching us more than themselves. I smell success," he halfheartedly observed.

"Your plan is working," she complimented him.

"Which plan?" He twirled her again and back into his arms.

"You are really getting into this. Have you been drinking?"

Gloria laughed, as he twirled her around again.

"Yes. Drinking up the sight of your beauty makes me intoxicated with joy."

They both started laughing so hard that they almost had to stop dancing.

While Gloria and Ralph were still on the dance floor, Debbie asked Stewart, "Did you have trouble finding a tuxedo?"

"I didn't even look. It's just for one night. Why waste the money on something you only wear once?"

"I guess you have a point."

"I'm surprised to see Gloria looking so nice; I mean different tonight. I didn't mean for it to come out like that. You look okay too, I mean I'm used to you looking nice."

"Maybe we should change the subject," an irritated Debbie quipped.

Just then a young waiter came by and brushed up against Debbie's right shoulder in passing. Debbie instinctively jumped up, and with one karate swing of her hand, knocked the tray out of the waiter's hand, knocked the waiter down onto the standing table with dirty dinner plates flying all over the floor.

"I'm so sorry. Let me help you up," she said. By this time several other waiters rushed over to assist their fellow waiter off the floor and clean up the mess.

"We've got him, Debbie. Thanks," a waiter said, who was helping the struck waiter.

"I'm truly sorry," Debbie said again apologetically.

"No harm done," the half dazed waiter said as he staggered out with the assistance of the other waiters.

"What did you do that for?" Stewart said in amazement.

"I wasn't thinking. Sometimes I react too swiftly when my space is invaded," Debbie said.

Stewart moved his chair an inch or two away. Debbie was annoyed at his insensitive response.

"I'm not going to bite you."

"It's not your bite that I'm worried about."

"That was just a fluke accident."

"Let's drop the subject before you have another fluke accident."

The band switched to a slow moving number. Since Gloria and Ralph were already on the dance floor, Ralph took Gloria into his arms and ever so gently, brushed back her long full auburn hair with his fingers so that he could gaze into her lovely face. "I'm finding it very hard to resist the smell of your sweet smelling perfume," he softly spoke in her ear.

"I feel so safe, so comfortable, so in your arms," Gloria whispered. The music stopped but they kept dancing. "We'd better get back to the table. The program will begin soon," she said to him.

"Yes. We must not stay too long, although it seemed so short," he said as he escorted her back to their table.

Back at the table Ralph asked Stewart and Debbie, "Having a great time?"

"Great time," Stewart said stiffly.

"Great," Debbie tersely added. Stewart was sitting about a foot further away from Debbie.

Timothy returned to the podium to begin the presentation of awards. "It is my great pleasure to present an award for the most congenial pet, 'Talker' who talks to everyone. He is truly the friendliest mixer among us. Will Ralph please come and accept the award for your pet?"

"Talker? I'm so surprised. I never won an award before, even if it is for my pet. Thank you. I humbly accept this on behalf of Talker."

"I guess he gets his gift of gab from his owner," Gloria said to Ralph as she congratulated Ralph with a slow moving rub on his back.

"Our next award goes to the pet with the best even-tempered, mild-mannered spirit, and the award goes to two pets this year, they are the Goldies," Timothy announced.

Gloria went up to the stage and accepted the award.

"Thank you. I will always cherish this award for the Goldies."

"How swimmingly fantastic that your pets won an award.

You deserve one too, the way you took such good care of your goldfish. You'd make a wonderful mother," Ralph smiled as he respectfully kissed Gloria on her hand.

"Our next award goes to the most adventurous pet. Though many pets here did many things, there can be no doubt that Butter was the most daring in many ways."

Debbie took Butter with her to the stage, and said, "On behalf of Butter and myself, thank you for this award. I don't think of her as adventurous. She's just had a few mishaps this week. Thank you for the award anyway."

Stewart commented to Debbie, "Are we talking about the same Butter?"

Debbie refused to respond.

"Our last but not least award goes to what we call the 'Most Valuable Pet' award for the pet who has exemplified the ideals and principles that we try so hard to emulate here at Pets-by-the-Sea Hotel. This pet has gone above and beyond the call of faithfulness to his master. He was not only obedient, dependable and unselfish, he also saved not only Butter from drowning, but he also saved the lives of many pets. In addition, he saved my mother from the kidnappers and he saved this hotel from the People Against Pets. Let's give a standing ovation as Bread comes up to receive this award for 'Most Valuable Pet.'"

Without any further prompting, all the guests and hotel staff stood and applauded Bread as he and Stewart made their way up to the stage. The musicians played "Pets Are For People," in honor of Bread being a true hero to all of them.

"Speech, speech, speech," yelled the audience.

Stewart started to speak, but someone in the audience yelled, "Bread. We want to hear from Bread."

Stewart lowered the mike to Bread.

Bread said, "Bark, Bark, Bark, Bark," as he waved his tail in gratitude.

Sensing that Bread had said it all, Stewart returned to his seat with Bread.

Unfortunately, Debbie was not as impressed by Stewart's silence.

"You should have said something up there," Debbie complained.

"Like what? Bread said it all," a perturbed Stewart asked.

"A simple 'thank you' would have been nice," she chided him.

"I think that's what Bread said," he grumbled.

Gloria and Ralph watched Stewart and Debbie argue, while they sat in silence.

Debbie, in disgust, got up and ran out of the Banquet Hall in tears with Butter not far behind on her leash. She saw Abby while outside on the terrace.

Abby noticed her sad mood and asked, "What's the matter, dear?"

"Hi Abby. I'm just confused right now."

"Confused about what?"

"I thought I liked one guy, and then when I saw the guy that I dumped, having fun with another woman, I think I like him. The guy I'm with tonight has faults, while the other guy seems so perfect. How did I miss this?"

"All that seems perfect rarely is. At least you know what the faults are in the guy you're with," she explained.

Abby continued, "Did you just meet the guy you are with tonight, this week?"

"Yes. I really like him, or at least I thought I did. I really don't know now," Debbie tearfully confided.

"Tell me, are you perfect?" Abby asked.

With a smile on her face Debbie knew she was not perfect.

"You can't keep karate chopping every guy that wants to talk to you."

"I know. I'm just so afraid to get close. I've been hurt before."

"It can be a scary world out there. Let God lead you and guide you. God wants you to be happy, not sad. Now dry your eyes and go back inside and just enjoy the evening. Most of all, God wants you to live life. Go my child and live."

Debbie gave Abby a hug and "thanks."

By now, Stewart had been sitting alone for several minutes.

He got up and went to the restroom. On his way back, he ran into David.

"Excuse me Stewart, but I couldn't help but notice that you and Debbie are a little on edge tonight. Is there something I can help you with?"

"Not really. I wouldn't know what kind of help I needed anyway," Stewart said despondently. "Debbie seemed ticked off and I don't know why," a puzzled Stewart commented.

"I've seen these kinds of things before. If two people are meant for each other, God will find a way to show them how to stay together. Mind if I give you a little advice from a man that's been happily married for over thirty years?" David offered.

"What's that?"

"Keep the big picture in mind. Don't let the ups and downs of life get you off course of what is important in life. Sometimes you have to grow in wisdom. It doesn't happen overnight."

"I know what's important in life. I've got Bread, man's best friend, my dog, and I've got bread, because I know how to bake it, and I've got bread, in that I make enough money to keep me comfortable for the rest of my life. I've got it all. I don't need anybody," Stewart boasted.

"My dear son, man does not live by bread alone. He needs love and meaningful relationships. Money won't keep you warm at night."

"What are you trying to say? I should stay with Debbie?"

"Not exactly. Some things don't reveal themselves in just one week. Pray on it, give it time, and the Lord will lead you in the right direction."

"Lord knows I don't want to mess up my life or anyone else's. I just never saw Gloria the way she was tonight."

"One night does not make a relationship for a lifetime. In a quiet time of solitude with the Lord, ask Him."

"But what if the Lord doesn't answer my prayer?"

"He always answers prayer. The breakdown in communication is when man doesn't listen to the answer," David clarified.

"Thanks for the advice. I'm listening," Stewart shook David's hand before returning to the Banquet room.

Upon Stewart's return to the table, Debbie sat quietly.

Ralph and Gloria left the table to dance.

"Can we talk?" Debbie opened up first. "I had no

idea I was going to meet someone like you when I came to Savannah.

It's all so overwhelming, the emotions and all."

"What are you trying to say, Debbie?" he somberly asked.

"I don't know if I can handle this right now. I've never met anyone like you that I'm so attracted to that my usual defenses aren't working well. Maybe we should cool it. I need to sort this out with the Lord's help. Do you know what I mean?"

Debbie said candidly.

"Yes, I do. I think we both need to pray on this, Debbie.

Can I have your telephone number in Detroit, just in case the Lord says yes about us?"

"Let me think about it. Can I have your phone number, instead?"

"I'll let you know. I did not come here for a commitment.

It was not part of my plans," Stewart defensively said.

"Your plans? Or the Lord's?" Debbie asked cynically.

Catching herself as being too judgmental, Debbie regrouped and said, "This is our last night together. Let's dance," Debbie tried not to make the moment any more difficult than it was.

"Yes. Let's do that."

The song was a slow dance.

Gloria told Ralph, "This may be our last night together, but somehow, I don't want the night to end."

"Neither do I." He held her closer as though he never wanted to let her go. Gloria reciprocated by moving her hands to the back of his head gently caressing his freshly cut wavy dark hair.

"There is something I want to tell you. It's very important to me," Gloria said looking Ralph in the eye.

"What's that, sweetheart?"

She closed her eyes and held him gently as they continued to dance. In an ever so soft, barely audible voice she whispered, "I'm a virgin."

Ralph stopped and looked at her with an equally sincere voice, "I never thought I'd tell anyone this."

"Tell someone what?"

"So am I. Shush. I have an image to maintain." With that confession, he twirled her around and at arms length, before he twirled her back into his arms to continue the dance.

Absently Gloria asked Ralph, "What are they doing now?" referring to Debbie and Stewart.

Ralph softly whispered in her ear, "I hadn't noticed."

Debbie, felt the pressure of making a decision immediately delayed. She found herself relaxing a little. Stewart seemed relaxed too, as they continued to dance.

"You are so beautiful, inside and out," he commented gazing into Debbie's eyes and then resumed holding her close.

"I'll always remember you in my heart," she said as she rested her head on his shoulders. The music picked up to a lively beat, as the finale to a memorable evening. On the dance floor were David and Abby. David showcased his fancy dance steps. Abby was trying her best to keep up with him. They were out-dancing everyone else on the floor, having a grand celebration of a time, as the musicians played "Live, Live, Live!"

Wake up and live.

Get up and live.

Live, live, live.

Live for love.

Live for right.

Live, live, live.

You won't regret,

A just led life.

Live, live, live.

Wake up and live.

Get up and live.

Live, live, live.

"All this dancing is working up an appetite," David said to his wife.

"I've got Girard keeping an extra plate of food hot for you," Abby said.

"Thanks." He continued dancing with more exuberance.

Ralph and Gloria were dancing pretty lively too. Bread and Butter were enjoying the adulations around the room, as well as snacks.

Stewart and Debbie didn't notice the celebration as they danced slowly to the beat of their hearts. Eventually, the music stopped. The evening was over.

27

Everyone who was leaving the hotel that Saturday morning was in the lobby to take the hotel shuttle vans to the Savannah International Airport. The guests were on one van and the large pets were on another.

Debbie approached Ralph who was already seated and asked, "Mind if I sit next to you?"

"No. Go right ahead."

"Where is Talker?" Debbie inquired.

"I came here with just my drumsticks, and that's all I'm leaving with. I gave Talker to Timothy."

"I'm sure Timothy will enjoy Talker."

"Yeah."

Next, Gloria got on the bus and saw Debbie with Ralph.

She kept walking past them for a seat.

Lastly, Stewart arrived. He saw Debbie sitting with Ralph and kept walking past them for the empty seat by Gloria.

"Hi, Gloria. Is this seat taken?" Stewart asked.

"No."

"So what are you going to do with your Goldies when you get back?"

"I gave them to Martha."

"That's nice."

"Looks like everyone is here on the van," Timothy announced as he walked down the aisle.

Just before the van left, David and Abby got on.

David gave a final farewell. "On behalf of the entire staff at our Pets-by-the-Sea Hotel, we hope you enjoyed your stay and wish you all a safe trip home. We certainly were blessed by your presence, and hope that you will return to visit us again. God bless you all."

"We love you," Abby added. Then David and Abby exited the bus.

While waiting at the airport gate, Debbie looked down at her ticket seat number and remembered it was next to Stewart.

She really didn't feel comfortable with that thought.

"Here. I'd like to switch the seat tickets with you, so that you can sit next to Stewart," Debbie somberly said to Gloria.

Gloria switched the tickets and just as somberly said, "Thanks."

Gloria's airplane ticket, which Debbie now had, was next to Ralph.

"Please fasten your seat belts. We will be taking off in a few minutes for Detroit."

Stewart chatted with Gloria. "Even though we've worked together for awhile, I know very little about you, other than your work, which is very good by the way," Stewart opened.

"What is it that you want to know?"

"Do you like food? I guess that was a dumb question," Stewart apologetically asked.

"Sometimes. Can I ask you a question?" Gloria laughed.

"Of course."

"Do you like clothes? I mean, fancy shorts, the kind that Ralph wore," she asked.

"Not much, except Debbie wore some really nice clothes last week," Stewart pondered out loud.

He took a deep breath and continued, "I saw a side of you that I never saw before last night. Maybe when we get back to Detroit, we can go out for dinner or something?"

"Okay. That would be nice," Gloria politely, but halfheartedly said.

Debbie and Ralph were seated some distance from Stewart and Gloria.

Debbie turned to Ralph and commented, "I saw a different person last night in that tuxedo. You should wear them more often."

"Thanks, but they would be just a little bit confining when I'm playing my drums," Ralph laughed.

"I guess so," Debbie laughed back.

"Anyway," she continued, "What else do you do besides play drums?"

"Sleep. That is, unless I'm on a date, then I don't sleep," he joked.

"I don't think we've ever completed a date. Maybe we could try that again?" she suggested.

"Good idea," he said.

The airplane flight attendant offered drinks and sandwiches to the passengers.

"What would you like to drink?" she asked Gloria.

"I'll have some Fizzle, thanks. Ralph used to joke around when we ordered beverages."

"And you sir?"

"Can I have two of them? And make those two sandwiches also, since they are free."

"Yes sir."

"What would you like to drink?" the attendant asked when she got to Ralph.

"You got something strong in there?" Ralph joked.

"As a matter of fact, we do."

"Then keep it. Just asked. I'll take Smooth Taste on the rocks."

"Just water for me please," Debbie said.

"See this Smooth Taste pop looks like scotch. That way I get to look like I'm drinking when I'm not," Ralph explained to Debbie.

"What about the bubbles?" Debbie asked looking at the fizz from the pop.

"I use lots of ice to hide that. Come to think of it, I never explained that to Gloria."

"Looks like we're almost there," Debbie said looking out the window as the plane circled to land at Detroit.

"Ralph," she said. "I really don't think it would be fair of me to date you when I've got someone else on my mind.

Actually, I'm not sure whom I have on my mind. Would it be okay if I took a little time to sort things out before we dated?" she humbly asked.

Ralph took a deep breath. "Yeah. You know where I

live. Call me when you're ready. I wouldn't want to rush things either. I understand."

Somewhat surprised at his considerate words, all Debbie could say was, "Thanks."

Stewart noted, "I've completely forgotten about the office this past week. I've got to call Monzie to pick me up. Do you have a ride home, Gloria?"

"Yes. My friend Sharon will pick me up. I'll see you at the office on Monday."

"Okay. I'll see you later," he acknowledged.

The attendant announced on the speaker, "We are now preparing to land. Please make sure your seats are fully upright and your seatbelts are firmly fastened."

The airplane pilot came on the speaker, "The temperature in Detroit is a cool 70 degrees and cloudy. We hope you enjoy your stay in Detroit. Thank you for flying Comfy Airlines."

The airline jingle played one last time, "We care about you, way up in the sky. Whether humans or pets, we go where you fly."

"Hi Sis. How was the flight?" Will hugged Debbie.

"There certainly wasn't a dull moment. Thanks for picking me up at the airport."

"No problem. The car is right over here." Debbie settled into the car with Butter in her arms.

A few minutes into the drive down the freeway, she asked Will, "How do you know if someone is really right for you?"

"You don't know, but God knows. Why do you ask? Did you like the guy you met down there?"

"Butter had a good time." Debbie returned to the

subject on her heart. "I don't even know if he likes me. Its so hard to tell if a man really loves you or is just playing a game trying to get into bed with you."

"Sis, with time, the truth will eventually be revealed to you, either by his actions or the Holy Spirit."

"The truth is that I think I love him."

"So when are you going to see him again?"

"We won't. I told him I didn't want to date guys right now."

"It sounds like you're willing to make one exception."

"I don't even have his phone number. And then there is Ralph, the other guy."

"Ralph, the drummer? I thought you threw him, literally, out of your life?"

"Yes and no. I may have thrown them both out."

"Whoa, you do have a dilemma. Sometimes God has a way of choosing what's best for us, even when we don't know what to ask for."

"Thanks, Will."

Stewart, having called Monzie to pick him up, was standing on the curb of the arrival section of the airport terminal, looking down the freeway in the direction that he had seen Debbie leave. Monzie approached him.

"Hey, buddy. Been gone that long that you don't even recognize your boss?" Monzie joked.

"Hi. It's good to see you," Stewart said, still distracted and gazing into the distance.

"I had a chance to drop by the office before I picked you up. It's still where we left it," Monzie joked again.

"That's nice."

"You haven't heard a word I've said."

"I'm sorry. What did you say?"

"Did you find any good real estate deals in Savannah? I know you didn't go to Savannah without doing some work."

"Didn't look."

"No? Did you catch up on your e-mail and computer file management?"

"No. Not enough time."

"No time? You had a whole week. What did you do?" Monzie reached over to touch Stewart on the forehead. "Are you sick?"

Turning his head away Stewart calmly stated, "We had a boat ride and we took a bus tour of the city. Things like that."

"We?" Monzie's ear leaned closer to Stewart.

"Bread was with me," Stewart clarified.

"That 'we' was a woman. I can tell," Monzie figured.

Silence. "Okay, who is she?"

"I don't want to talk about it."

"Fine with me," Monzie said as he continued driving down the freeway for a few miles.

Without an answer to his previous question, Monzie spoke again, "When do I get to meet her?"

"You won't. I'm never going to see her again."

"Why?"

"In the first place, we had a fight on the last night. In the second place, even if I wanted to see her I don't have her telephone number. And in the third place, even if I had her number, she doesn't want to see me again."

"She actually told you that?"

"Yes, no. Not in those exact words. Besides, I started dating someone else."

"Wow. Two women in one week. Aren't you the lucky guy?"

Monzie smiled.

"Lucky me," Stewart said with no enthusiasm in his words.

"Who is she, I mean the second one?"

"Gloria."

"Gloria who?"

"You know. Our Gloria."

"Our Gloria, your secretary?" a surprised Monzie asked.

The silence resumed as they went a few more miles up the freeway.

"She's a nice kid. Which one do you love?"

"What kind of question is that?"

"Hold on. I'm sorry, I didn't mean to pry."

"That's what you've been doing since I got in this car."

Ignoring that last comment Monzie offered a bit of advice.

"Man, take it from one who has been married for thirty-five wonderful years to the same terrific woman and six beautiful children later. Better choose the right one."

"The choice has already been made," Stewart concluded.

"By whom?"

"Not me."

"The choice is yours too. Besides, I don't want you to hurt Gloria. Lord knows she's had her share of rejections in the office alone. Do me one favor, man."

"What's that?"

"Level with Gloria. Be straight with her."

"Okay. I'll do that."

"There's my house. Thanks for the lift. Here's a little something for gas."

"Something did happen to you all right. I'll take a rain ticket on the gas money. See you at work on Monday."

Gloria's ride from Sharon came to the airport.

"I can hardly wait to hear what happened in Savannah.

How did you do? Did you catch Stewart like you planned?"

Sharon asked.

"Yes," Gloria flatly said.

"Yes? Congratulations! Child you should be jumping for joy. Let's celebrate. I know this great new café we can go to after you unpack. Then you can tell me all about it."

"I really don't feel like celebrating. I think I'll just stay in tonight."

"What? You always want to party. Okay. What's wrong?"

"Nothing."

"I've known you too long. What happened?"

"I got Stewart, but..."

"But what? He turned out to be an unsavory character?"

"No. He was a gentleman. I met this other guy while I was down there. He got with someone else, someone that he is crazy about. Anyway, I got Stewart and I should be happy, but I have these feelings that I can't explain."

"Look girlfriend. I know Stewart has a lot of money, even if he is a little tight with it. I know that he is a very good looking man, but if you are not happy with him, all the money and good looks and even gentlemanly ways won't mean a thing if you don't love him."

"I thought I loved him. Maybe I still do?"

"Don't string Stewart along. He deserves to be number one, not two, in a woman's life."

"Who said he was number two, can't he tie for first place?"

Gloria laughed.

"I won't answer that question. Is this other guy married?

"Of course not."

"Then there's always hope."

"You're right. I'll just have to find a way to let Stewart down gently."

"By the way, not to change the subject, our church choir is scheduled to sing at the Blest Fest next Saturday at the Hart Plaza and the choir director wants you to sing a solo."

"Next Saturday? That's only a week away."

"I know. Our director has us scheduled to rehearse every night this week."

"I don't know if I'll attend. I don't feel up to praising the Lord right now. I don't feel very blessed either."

"Child, if I had soap, I'd wash your mouth out. Listen to you. That's all the more reason to get out. I'll pick you up at 6:00 p.m. on Monday for rehearsal."

"Okay, I didn't mean to say that. I'm just tired right now."

"You go get some rest. I'll see you in church tomorrow."

"Bye. Thanks for the ride and the advice."

Gloria barely put down her luggage when she heard her phone ring.

"Gloria? It's Stewart."

"Yes. It's me."

"I've been thinking, I'm a little confused right now. I don't think this is the right time to date you. However, I want you to know that I think you are a very nice person. I wouldn't want to lead you on."

"I was thinking the same thing too, Stewart."

"You were? Somehow, I didn't expect this to go so smoothly. You okay?"

"I'm fine. See you Monday. We'll probably have a lot of work waiting for us after a week away."

"Right. See you at work."

Ralph's brother, Ethan, had arrived at the airport for him.

"How was the trip, man?" Ethan asked.

"Don't ask. Where are my drums?" an irritated Ralph asked.

"Back in your apartment. And it's nice to see you too," Ethan said expressing his displeasure at such a cold greeting.

"I'm sorry, Ethan. Thanks for picking me up at the airport and taking care of my drums. What's happening?"

Ethan cautiously informed Ralph, "Through a connection, I hooked up a gig while you were on vacation."

"That's great. Where?" Ralph smiled.

"The Blest Fest at the Hart Plaza," Ethan said quietly.

"The what?" Ralph shouted. "Isn't that church stuff?"

"It's a concert of traditional and contemporary Christian music."

"I don't care what it is. Do I look like a choir boy?"

"I've picked some really nice pieces for us to play. We need to expand our repertoire," Ethan reasoned.

"Okay, little brother. I guess a gig is a gig. How much do we get paid?"

Silence.

"It's okay, I wouldn't expect much from a church thing.

How much, man?"

"It's free."

"The concert is free! I know you are not talking about us playing for free?"

"We play for free, but its good publicity," Ethan

rationalized.

"What? I don't get this," Ralph fussed.

Ethan looked straight ahead as he drove down the freeway, not saying a word.

The silence continued for another five minutes.

"I don't know why I'm doing this, but you said we'd do it and I'm a man of my word." Ralph reluctantly agreed.

Ethan was not smiling. "There's another tiny detail or two that I need to know."

"I'm afraid to ask. What?" Ralph's irritation rekindled.

"We couldn't, or I didn't think it was a good idea to play at the Blest Fest with a name like 'Rolling with Ralph.' So I changed the name, just for the concert, to 'Ralph and the Righteous.'"

"You did what? What has gotten into you? I put you in charge of the band for one week and you get a *free* gig to play *church* music, and now you've changed the name?"

"Dad thought it was a good idea," Ethan explained.

"Of course he would. He's a pastor. Why wouldn't he want his sons to have a name like righteous?" Ralph threw up his hands in disgust.

"Then we're all set," Ethan ended.

"Change it back," Ralph ordered.

"It's too late. It's already gone to the printer. Remember, this is good publicity."

"What good is good publicity if you've got the wrong name?" Ralph fumed.

"It's just for one day. After that, we can go back to 'Rolling with Ralph.' I've never asked you for anything before. Trust me on this."

"I know you've basically done everything I've asked without complaining once. Okay, but don't tell any of my friends."

"I won't tell a soul," Ethan smiled.

"As soon as this gig is over, we are going back to the name, 'Rolling with Ralph.' I've got an image to maintain."

28

Monday, two days after the Savannah trip, everybody returned to their routines.

While waiting at home for Stewart to return from work, Bread looked out the front window of the house and saw a stray cat scampering down the street. It was not Butter, so he returned to his dog bed. He turned on the TV by pushing a button with his paw and looked at a cartoon show of a cat and dog trying to figure out how to get through a maze in a game.

Butter kept Debbie's apartment undisturbed since she returned from the trip, leaving very little for the housekeeper, Ms. Flowers, to straighten up.

"How are you feeling, Butter? You're not as active as you were before the trip."

Butter sat with her head bowed down.

That evening Debbie met with her group, SafeCity.

One member, Lydia, updated Debbie. "You would be so proud of us. We've had one testy conflict after another while you were away on vacation. You will be happy to know that we behaved admirably, just like you would, rationally and peacefully," Lydia beamed with the good news. Debbie's eyes started to swell with tears. She was unable to contain the big teardrops that fell down her cheeks.

"What's wrong?" Lydia asked. "Did we say something to upset you?"

"I have a confession to make. I'm a very violent person. I didn't realize it until it was too late," Debbie cried as her lips quivered.

"You don't look violent to us, dear."

"I only get that way when I'm approached by a man," she sobbed.

"That explains it. I mean, things will work itself out. We all have weaknesses, dear. Just remember, God told us in Second Corinthians 12:9: *'My grace is sufficient for thee: for my strength is made perfect in weakness.'* God has a way of turning our mistakes into masterpieces. Trust Him. Okay?"

"I will. I've tried everything else." Debbie wiped the tears from her face.

The next day, Tuesday morning, Stewart was buried in his work back at Detroit Prime Properties, Inc. While going through some papers that he had taken on the trip, but never got around to reading, he found a picture of Debbie that he had taken with his disposable camera on the night of the Awards Banquet.

"She looked so stunning and I blew it."

Gloria walked into his office.

"Hi, Stewart. Here is the letter to be signed," she flatly said.

Stewart looked down at the stapler she had handed him instead of the letter.

"Gloria, I think this is yours and the letter in your other hand is for me to sign."

"Oops. Here's your letter. Your client is here for his appointment."

"Thanks. Send him in, please."

"Good morning, Stewart. Just call me Angelo." The real estate tycoon sat down at the small conference table with Stewart. "I've got a vision to purchase the Hart Plaza so that I can preserve the family gatherings by bringing in more wholesome family entertainment."

"You realize that currently the festivals are free? I seriously doubt if you could make a profit at such an expensive venture without charging the visitors. Would you like our office to work up a cost and income analysis?"

"Yes, up to a point. I'm not going to charge an entrance fee either."

"Then how, Angelo, are you going to make a profit?"

"Son, I've made more money in my various ventures than I could spend in a lifetime, without wasting it. My vision is to share my wealth. You know what the Bible says?"

Stewart squirmed. "No, what does the Bible say?" "Matthew 16:26 says: *'For what is a man profited, if he shall gain the whole world and lose his own soul? or what shall a man give in exchange for his soul?'*"

Stewart cleared his throat, "How much does it cost for a soul?"

"Nothing, and everything, Son. Jesus paid it all."

"Then making money is free and clear, the way I see it, minus tithing."

"Not exactly. First Timothy 6:17-19 says: *'Charge them that are rich in this world, that they be not highminded, nor trust in uncertain riches, but in the living God, who giveth us richly all things to enjoy; That they do good, that they be rich in good works, ready to distribute, willing to communicate; Laying up in store for themselves a good foundation against the time to come, that they may lay hold on eternal life.'* That means share the wealth, son, with good causes. That's not all."

"Don't tell me there is more?"

"Glad you asked. Yes, First Corinthians 13:3 says: *'And though I bestow all my goods to feed the poor, and though I give my body to be burned, and have not love, it profiteth me nothing.'* Get it?"

"Yes. Give it."

"With love. Without love, there's no life."

Stewart looked at Debbie's picture still in view on his desk.

"It's not easy for me to give up money. My family was poor. I remember growing up so hungry that we ate the dandelion leaves in our yard. We were so poor that when the teacher told us students in class about the old lady whose cupboards were bare, I thought she was talking about my family."

"Whom do you trust? Your money or God to keep you from going hungry again?"

"God of course, technically speaking, but money rings in my ear, saying 'Money will save you from the bill collectors.'"

"Only God can save. We are just his instruments. Proverbs 3:5-6 says: *'Trust in the Lord with all thine heart; and lean not unto thine own understanding. In all thy ways acknowledge him, and he shall direct thy paths.'* Trust His love to show you the way."

"Trust Love," Stewart pensively said as his shoulders visibly relaxed.

"You've got it! This weekend, there's a Blest Fest at Hart Plaza for which I need a visual assessment for my accountants."

Monzie walked into Stewart's office. "Hello Angelo."

"Hi Monzie. I believe Stewart is the man for this job. Nice meeting you. Your firm can take care of all the details."

"We sure will. Take care."

Monzie picked up where Angelo left off.

"We've got the legal description of the property and some breakdown of all of the festival's financial statements; however, we need a person to actually view the property. We also need a person to observe one of the festivals to see what type of services and benefits to the community are being generated firsthand," he explained to Stewart. "I want you to check it out for me. You have an eye for combining costs with use of property. After you do that, we will put everything together for our client."

"Okay boss. When do you need it?"

"I told them that I would get back to them by next Monday."

"That's a pretty short notice. It only leaves one weekend, this Saturday."

"I know. Most of the other staff is busy with family commitments, myself included. I figured you're probably not doing anything much over the weekend. Plus, we need to move on this quickly before news gets out. We've got another multimillion dollar commission riding on this."

"You've got a point, Monzie. I wasn't planning anything and this deal could easily become a high publicity item like the last one. I'll spend Saturday checking out the place and event. I'll take Bread with me so as not to look too conspicuous."

"Good idea. Maybe the fresh air will be good for you and Bread. You've been looking kind of sad since your trip. Oops.

There goes my cell phone. The wife and I are going out to dinner tonight at that new restaurant downtown, 'Sweet Times.' Got to go."

That Wednesday, while sorting through the daily mail, Stewart came across a solicitation for money from a local homeless shelter. He usually tossed such requests without reading it. They were requesting $5, $25 or "other" to help cover the expenses of the shelter. He reached for his pen and checked off "other." He took his checkbook and with trembling hands he wrote a check for $10,000. "It's the least I can do."

He picked up the telephone. "Gloria, would you come in here for a moment, please."

Gloria returned to his office.

"Please mail this for me."

Gloria looked at the printed name on the outside of the envelope. "Stewart, you usually toss these kinds of things in the waste basket."

"Do you think I'm cheap?" he asked her.

"How much was the donation?"

"$10,000."

"No. Not at all. I'll mail this right away." He was still holding an edge of the envelope as she pulled it out of his fingers.

"Boss, I need to find something to wear for the weekend. Can I take a little extra time on my lunch hour?"

"Go right ahead."

She went into the "New You" store.

"May I help you?" the boutique owner asked.

"Yes. I'm looking for something to wear at a Christian concert this weekend. What do you suggest?"

"I'm Angelo, the owner. I'm filling in for my sales manager today. We have some lovely summer outfits on sale over here."

"I don't see anything that I usually wear. I like to wear more revealing clothes, but I'll look anyway, since I don't have much time.

"Did you say Christian concert?"

"Yes. I did."

"Then you'll want to wear something conservative. How about this?"

"I want something beautiful. Outstanding. Something that will grab attention."

"Daughter, beauty is from within. Are you saved?"

"I think so."

"Let's find a nice outfit, which will preserve your beauty. We don't want the whole world to see you. Save a little mystery for that special someone."

"I don't have a special someone."

"In that case, save it all."

"Angelo, if I don't dress sexy, people won't like me."

"Who are you inside, Gloria, whom you are trying to cover up?"

"I overheard my parents, when I was a child, tell my sisters that they were prettier than me. I'm ugly, that's who I am," she said with her head bowed down.

Angelo bent his head down, to catch her eyes. She lifted her head up a little.

"You are God's child, made in His image. Is God ugly?"

"I've never seen Him."

"The Bible describes God in Psalm 90:17 which says: *'And let the beauty of the Lord our God be upon us.'* Do you know what's really important to God? Matthew 5:16 says: *'Let your light so shine before men, that they may see your good works, and glorify your Father which is in heaven.'* You can shine with glitter from the inside out."

"Spiritual glitter? How intriguing. That will really trick them."

"God does not like deceits. Truthfulness, honesty and integrity, that's what He wants."

"He's asking a lot."

"He gave a lot. He thought you were worth sending his Son, Jesus Christ, to die for your salvation."

"I've really messed up then. I did some pretty deceitful things on my vacation last week. I'll never be in God's graces."

"He forgives all of our faults, if we would turn from our sinful ways and repent."

"That won't be easy, especially since that person I harmed was my boss."

"If it will make you feel any better, I'm sure God will send an angel to look out for you and him. You really should talk to your boss today."

"Okay. I also need a few accessories. Let me see your shoes."

"*'How beautiful are the feet of them that preach the gospel of peace, and bring glad tidings of good things!'* That's in Romans 10:15," Angelo quoted.

"Gee. You know a lot of scripture."

Gloria returned to work after a two-hour lunch break.

"Stewart, got a minute?"

"Sure, Gloria. What is it?"

"I owe you an apology. I did some pretty dishonest things while on vacation. To make matters worse, I brought Ralph in to help me hurt you and Debbie. It you want to fire me, I'd understand." Gloria stood with her eyes tightly shut.

"Gloria, I eventually saw what you and Ralph were up to. If I had my act together, I wouldn't have been so swayed by the challenges. I think we both learned some hard lessons. I forgive you. You can keep your job. After all, that's what David Shepherd taught us.

"Thanks boss, I'll work an extra hour tonight to make up for the long lunch hour."

"If it will make you feel better, okay, but it won't be necessary. My main concern is how to see Debbie again. She didn't want to give me her phone number. Have you heard from Ralph?"

"Last we saw Ralph, he was sitting with Debbie. They probably forgot all about us."

It was late Thursday, two days before the concert. Ralph tossed restlessly, unable to sleep. He flipped the channels on his digital cable TV.

"Today's TV topic is about birds, parakeets, as a matter of fact. Did you know that parakeets make great pets?"

"Talker was all right," Ralph said as he flipped the

TV off entirely.

Still awake, Ralph decided to practice on his drums in his one bedroom Detroit Lofty Towers apartment. He had refused to practice with the band for the concert. He furiously pounded away on his drums. He flailed his tightly held drumsticks frantically making a horrendous noise. Finally, exhausted, large teardrops started to roll down his cheeks as he sobbed almost as loud as the drumbeats. He dropped the drumsticks to the floor. He bent down to the floor, face buried in his hands and on fallen knees, he said, "What have I done, Lord?"

Just at that moment, there was a knock outside of his apartment door.

"Whoever it is, go away," Ralph said loudly.

The knock on the door continued.

"Open up," said the man next door.

Ralph regrouped his composure, got up off his knees and opened the door a little.

"If you're complaining about the drums, I stopped."

"As a matter of fact, I was. I could hear that thing next door."

Ralph opened the door wider as he stood at the entrance.

"Sorry. I stopped. Now go on back to your apartment."

"You're crying. Let me in, please?"

"Shush. Come on in. The last thing I want is for everyone in the building to hear you say that."

"Thanks," said the neighbor.

"What's it to you? I don't even know you, beyond seeing you in the building."

"I know Jesus, and that's all you need to know. Maybe I can help."

"Help? Who asked for help? I'm fine."

"Yes. You are. I can tell you'll be just fine. I know this is awkward, but the Lord led me to knock on this door, and your drumming woke me up to hear Him."

"I know Jesus, but I don't think He wants any part of me for some terrible things I did last week."

"If you really knew Jesus, you'd know that he loves even the people who screw up."

"Getting love from God is one thing. That's nice. But how can those folks that I've hurt ever forgive me?"

"God can fix anything, even that, if you ask Him."

"I thought I was so tough that no one could get to my heart, but Gloria did. Now I'm paying the price for messing up Debbie and Stewart's thing. I would do anything to make it right between Debbie and Stewart and get Gloria back in my life."

"You can start with being humble."

"Humble? That's not part of my image. What if the chicks reject me, or worse, laugh at me?"

"'Fowl' comments are for chicks; excuse the pun. Loving words are for women. There will always be somebody who rejects you just because you're Christ's child. If you really want to be a tough guy, stand up for Christ. There's more than one way to be macho."

"I never thought of it that way. I can be strong for the Lord. Will he have my back?"

"Yes, He and His angels."

"Thanks. It was really nice of you to get up out of your bed to do this."

"Hey, I've got your back. Now get some rest. Good night," said the neighbor.

"It seems like my bad night just turned into a good night.

I didn't get your name."

"Angelo."

It was Friday, mid-morning. Debbie was working in her design studio office, "Debbie by Design." A customer arrived for his appointment to discuss designing his child's bedroom.

"Hi, I'm Angelo," he began. "My wife and I noticed that our little one just loves cats and dogs. Do you think you could decorate his room in a cat and dog motif? I know this might be an unusual request," he politely inquired.

"I can do that, Angelo. In fact, I've recently seen motifs with that theme, though I'll make your design much better."

"That would be great. Are you familiar with the Bible passage in Isaiah 11:6: *'The wolf also shall dwell with the lamb, and the leopard shall lie down with the kid; and the calf and the young lion and the fatling together; and a little child shall lead them.'* Can we get a mural in one corner of the room depicting that image?"

"Yes, a mural is doable. Just curious, how did that passage come to your mind?

"There is so much fighting in the world. We want our child to know that no matter how bad things are here on earth, that in the end, when Christ comes, there will be peace. You can understand that, can't you?"

"Definitely. Violence is everywhere, even where you least expect it. However, it's comforting to know that all these conflicts will ultimately pass."

"Comfort. That's the decorating message we want. Can you handle that?"

"Comfort? We could all use some comfort. I could use some comfort. Life can be so scary."

"Daughter, you shouldn't worry so much. The Father sent us a Comforter. Jesus said that the Father said in John 14:16-18: *'shall give you another Comforter, that he may abide with you forever; Even the Spirit of truth...ye know him; for he dwelleth with you, and shall be in you. I will not leave you comfortless; I will come to you.'* Your Comforter is with you 24/7."

"Somehow, I feel His presence taking a weight off of my shoulders."

"You never know when an angel may appear to guide you through tough times," Angelo said.

"Thanks. We'll focus on comfort for the ambiance of your child's room and for me when I start to feel threatened."

That Friday evening Debbie had just returned to her apartment after a long day in the office when the telephone rang. "Maybe Stewart found my number somehow?" she said to herself in anticipation.

"Hello, it's me, Will."

"Who?" Debbie asked.

"Your brother. I've been concerned about you all week.

Why don't you get out and have a little fun, Sis?"

"I don't know. Where? With who?" Debbie said listlessly.

"There must be something you can do. You live

downtown.

What about that Blest Fest at the Hart Plaza? It's going on this Saturday."

"I don't have anyone to go with me," Debbie said trying to come up with excuses not to do anything.

"You and Butter can walk over there for a nice sunny outing. What do you have planned for tomorrow?"

"Nothing. I guess the fresh air would be good for Butter.

She hasn't been out of the apartment since the trip."

"Great. You are going for sure?"

"Yes. I'll go for my brother."

"I'm flattered Sis, but this time, do it for Debbie."

"Okay."

Shortly thereafter, her phone rang.

"Maybe that's Stewart," she wondered out loud.

"Hi Debbie, it's Ralph."

"Oh, hi."

"I've got to get something off of my chest. I'm really sorry about screwing things up with you and Stewart. Have you heard from him?"

"No. Besides, he doesn't have my number."

"That's too bad. Please find a way to forgive me. This has really been bothering me."

"No. I should ask you to forgive me. If it weren't for me being so violent, I wouldn't have attacked you and Stewart like I did."

"No. You should forgive me. If I had respected your space and wishes, I never would have put you on the spot like that."

"No. There was no excuse for me flooring you like that. I am so sorry."

"Listen to us. We are two sorry people," he laughed.

"I'll accept your apology if you'll accept mine."

"It's a deal."

"Have you heard from Gloria?" she asked.

"No. She's probably with Stewart, like she planned."

"I guess. There's probably no point in me trying to find him. I thought about calling the travel agent."

"She was Gloria's best friend. Fat chance she'd give out the numbers," he said.

"What about information?"

"What city does he live in?"

"I never asked, but he works in Detroit."

"And who do you think will answer the phone?"

"His secretary, Gloria."

"I know this might sound strange coming from me, but one thing my dad taught me was when plans fail, pray fervently," he suggested.

"Bow your head." She prayed with Ralph.

Stewart was at home preparing his dinner. "Maybe her telephone is listed," he said to Bread. Stewart dialed the information operator. "Do you have a Deborah Dents listed?"

"That is a private number, sir."

"What about an interior design studio?"

"What is the name?"

"Debbie something, I'm not sure."

"Can't help you."

"Thanks." Stewart looked up interior designers in the yellow pages. "This must be it, "Debbie by Design." He called the number listed.

"Hello, Debbie by Design's hours are 9:00 a.m. to 5:00 p.m. Please leave a message."

Stewart hung up the phone. "What would I say?" He pushed redial. "It's Stewart Counts. Remember me? We met in Savannah last week."

The answering machine asked, "If you are not satisfied with this message, you may rerecord now."

He pushed the button to rerecord, but hung up before recording a message and looked at Bread. "If only I could see her face. I don't think I could take leaving a message and never hearing from her again."

Debbie was tired and went to bed early.

Butter quietly curled up to sleep in her cat's bed.

29

It was Saturday, early afternoon, one week after everyone had returned to Detroit from Savannah.

"Looks okay to me," Gloria said to herself while fixing her hair and checking her orange-red lipstick in the mirror of her car's visor, just before walking over to the Hart Plaza to sing in the Blest Fest choir.

"Miss Gloria," the choir director Joy Bells, said, upon seeing Gloria arrive in the holding area for performers before they took the stage. "Would you come over here please? Thank you," Joy motioned with her arms for Gloria to approach her.

"What is this?" Joy shook her finger at Gloria's robe's hemline.

"What? I just shortened it a little. It was too long," Gloria explained.

"A little? A little? Do you call six inches above your knees a little? Those four-inch loop earrings are a no-no." Ms. Bells shook her head.

"I always wear these earrings."

"Not in my choir. We are supposed to look uniform and understated in our appearance. Hand over the earrings and while you are at it, the bracelets and anklets too. I'll give them to the security staff to hold."

"But I'd feel underdressed without them."

"Better underdressed than too flashy. Get rid of them

right now. We are going on stage in a few minutes. Now hurry, hurry."

No one else wore large earrings and bangles.

"Okay. If I must."

Joy arranged the positions of the choir members.

"Everyone. Look at me. Look at me. Gloria, you stand behind the tall lady."

"But no one can see me," Gloria complained.

"Good."

Ethan and all of the "Ralph and the Righteous" band members were in place on the stage to the side, except for Ralph. The concert was ready to begin.

"Where is the band leader? We can't wait forever," Joy asked Ethan. Ethan shrugged his shoulders.

The Blest Fest master of ceremonies announced, "Our next act is by the Blest Fest Choir. Let's give a round of applause."

The audience politely applauded. Hearing the applause, Joy Bells had no choice but to begin. Ralph dashed to his drums.

"Where were you? You're late," Ethan chided his brother.

"Sorry, I got lost."

"You're found now. Let's roll."

Ralph wore a large rim hat and oversized dark glasses from his "Rollin with Ralph" band's outfit. He didn't have time to create a new image. Gloria missed a few cues since her view was blocked from seeing the director. Ralph also missed a few beats because he had not rehearsed with the choir. Joy Bells wasn't very joyful at her missed cues. She gave a look of disapproval to

Gloria and Ralph but they didn't notice her. Debbie arrived at the Hart Plaza seating area.

"Butter, I see an empty seat over there at the back. Come on and let's sit there in the far corner."

Stewart had just finished walking the long boardwalk by the Detroit River along the width of the Plaza. "I can see why someone would want to buy this place, Bread. It's spectacular.

This bright and sunny afternoon is a great family outing for those who have a family. Instead of going into the seating area, let's sit on the lawn up there under a shaded tree. We can still hear the music from that vantage point. I brought our homemade lunch and water, Bread. Here are a few biscuits for you."

The large gray-tone railing on the upper level blocked his view of the audience. Bread gulped the portable water Stewart had provided for him, after eagerly eating the biscuits.

The choir and band were into their second song.

Ralph kept missing beats.

Gloria kept singing off beat.

Debbie and Butter just sat.

Stewart and Bread just ate.

"My hair. Where did that drop come from?" Gloria asked as she looked up to the cloudless sky. Within minutes, a dark thundercloud rolled in creating a tremendous downpour of rain. Suddenly, everyone was running for cover.

"Butter, it's too far to run home. Let's go to the atrium, downstairs." Debbie quickly dashed for cover in the lower level of the Plaza. The shade tree under which Stewart and Bread sat gave no protection from the pouring rain. Stewart saw a lot of people heading to some back stairs to the lower level, where food vendors were located.

"Come on Bread. We've got to get away from these trees."

He followed the crowd down the stairs.

"Look at me. My hair is a mess," Gloria said while being ushered quickly off of the uncovered stage to a special indoor restaurant in the lower level that doubled as the performers' holding area. She ran to the restroom to get some paper towels to dry off. Ralph and the band were ushered into the same holding place as the choir. Ralph sat down at a bench while most of the performers ran around in confusion. While his back was turned, Gloria sat down at the same bench table with her back turned to him.

A teenaged volunteer helper came up to the water-drenched Ralph. "Would you like some water, sir?"

"No thanks. I'm wet enough. Got any drinks around here?"

The volunteer scampered off. Gloria turned around.

"They don't serve the kind of drink you're looking for at a Blest Fest."

Ralph turned around and saw Gloria.

"Gloria?" an almost speechless Ralph said.

"I see you remembered my name."

"I'll never forget it, ever," a mesmerized Ralph said as he got up, took Gloria by the hand, but instead of kissing her just yet he said, "There is something I want to say to you."

"And what is that?"

"I'm sorry for being such an insensitive, disrespectful guy during the vacation. I miss you so much. I hope you will give me a chance to show the real, nice guy in me. I honestly believe in honesty. It was really bothering me with the way we treated Debbie and Stewart and the way I treated you, too."

"Ralph, I knew you were a nice guy, somewhere, when you tried to help me that week in Savannah, but I didn't help matters either when I tried so hard to deceive Stewart and Debbie, too. I have to trust God to send me the right person without using fancy clothes and trickery."

"I believe in my heart that he has sent the right man to you, me. I love you, Gloria, for who you are, not what you are wearing. Your sweet spirit and joy are all the glitter I need."

"Me, too, I mean... Ralph, I love you. I believe I found my man, with a lot of help from God."

"Please don't break my heart, Gloria."

"You're safe with me."

"Let's dance." He took her hand.

"There's no music."

"When I'm with you, there's always music."

"Is that from the Song of Solomon?"

"No. From the Song of Ralph." Ralph took her in his arms and twirled her away from him, then twirled her back into his arms. They stopped, arms entangled around each other bringing their bodies so close that they could feel each other's heartbeat. They kissed their very first kiss, but not their last.

Just then, the volunteer returned, "Is Fresh Taste okay, sir?"

Gloria responded, "He'll take it." They both laughed.

Outside of the restaurant, in the covered atrium, the crowd was milling around. People were crowded together, bumping into each other. During the commotion, Debbie and Butter stood around and waited for the rain to stop. Underneath the feet of countless people running around for shelter from the rain, Butter's eye just barely caught a glimpse of a dog on the other side of the atrium. She took a second look and saw Bread. Without hesitation she made a mad dash, causing the wet leash to slip from Debbie's hand.

"Meow, meow," Butter yelled to Bread. Bread turned around and saw Butter running to him. He made an abrupt dash to Butter, causing Stewart to lose his grip of Bread's leash. There were so many people crowding into the area that they bumped into each other as they made their way through the crowd, never taking their eyes off each other. Bread licked Butter's face and Butter nudged back.

Debbie was frantically searched for Butter in the crowd.

"Butter, Butter, where are you?" She shouted, looking high and low.

Stewart rushed though the crowd looking for Bread.

"Bread. Where did you go? Bread? " He shouted through the crowd.

Finally, Debbie spotted Butter and rushed after her. When she reached down to pick up Butter, she saw Bread.

Debbie, barely able to speak, asked, "Bread? What are you doing here?"

Just then, Stewart found Bread standing there with Butter and Debbie. Debbie looked up. There was

Stewart.

"Debbie? Butter?" a surprised Stewart said blinking his eyes. "Is this a dream?"

"You're not dreaming, unless we're both dreaming."

"Debbie, you mean more to me than I ever thought possible.

All my money and career plans weren't enough to replace the love I feel for you.

Forgive me for acting like I was too rich to love."

"Stewart, I love you too. I didn't realize how violent I was until I thought about how I treated you and others. Please forgive me for being so hostile."

"We can both forgive each other. I understand it's scary trusting people."

Simultaneously, Stewart and Debbie just stood there, eyes locked on each other, oblivious to the rain outside. They allowed the jostling of the crowd to push them closer and closer together. Not more than two feet apart now, Butter and Bread, having had practice with these things before, instinctively grabbed their leashes and encircled Stewart and Debbie just a little, causing them to become closer as the leash entangled them. Joyfully, neither resisted. Their lips were just inches apart. Their bodies were almost touching. Their arms were still by their sides and motionless.

Butter leaned her side to Debbie, causing her to get within an inch of Stewart's lips. Likewise, Bread, leaned his side on Stewart, causing him to be one half inch from Debbie's.

"I need more than money in my life," he said.

"I need to trust God that you are the man for me," she replied.

Finally, both Bread and Butter were jumping on the back legs of Debbie and Stewart, respectively, pushing them to the inevitable. Stewart and Debbie kissed and embraced each other as they continued to kiss a very long kiss, oblivious to the world.

Bread and Butter jumped around with glee, in the middle of a crowd that barely noticed them.

Suddenly, the storm cloud rolled past and the loud speaker said, "We will resume the Blest Fest. The concert is starting again. You may return to your seats. Will the choir and musicians please return to the stage? Thank you."

Hand in hand Debbie and Stewart walked to their seats together with Butter and Bread trailing behind.

On their way to their seats, they saw Ralph and Gloria walking hand in hand to the stage.

"Ralph and Gloria?" Stewart asked.

"Hi guys. Meet my girlfriend," Ralph announced as he smiled at Gloria.

"That's fantastic. Meet my girlfriend," Stewart beamed with eyes fixed on Debbie.

"Give God the glory," Debbie joyfully shouted.

"Amen to that," Gloria cheerfully added.

"We've got a show to finish," Ralph said.

"And we've got a show to watch," Stewart laughed.

Gloria, whose turn it was to sing a solo, was finally permitted by the choir director to be seen by the audience. She sung joyfully with her heart and soul. Her eyes looked at Ralph.

Ralph got into the spirit of the moment, playing his drums with every fiber of his soul, as he looked at

Gloria.

Stewart and Debbie sat in the audience and clapped their hands as they swayed to the rhythm of the music.

Stewart waved at Gloria and Ralph. Gloria and Ralph waved back. Everyone in the audience was swinging to the music as the band and choir sung their final number, "God loves us all." The lyrics went,

> God loves us all
>
> And wants the best
>
> From each and all.
>
> That's why the test.
>
> When we forgive
>
> We show our love
>
> To all who live,
>
> And God above.

This time Gloria got all the words right and Ralph didn't miss a beat. Joy Bells busted out of her robe as she wildly directed the finale.

"That bottled water they're selling looks good," Debbie commented to Stewart.

"We'll take two bottles, please. How much?" he asked the vendor.

"$4.00 each sir."

The smallest bill Stewart had was a $50.

The vendor started to give Stewart his change.

"Keep the tip," he smiled.

"Thanks."

"How generous of you," Debbie noted.

He leaned over to her ear and whispered, "Sharing my life with you forever is more important to me than spending my money alone."

Stewart irresistibly raised his right arm behind Debbie's back and ever so gently lowered it on Debbie's right shoulder. She let his arm peacefully rest there. She nestled closer to him.

18893692R00151

Made in the USA
Charleston, SC
26 April 2013